"Ghoulish Good Fun"

'The Anthology Goes '*Bump*' In The Night'

by,

Robert A. Boyd

Cover illustration by Steven J Catizone

"Introduction"

Ah! I see we have another brave soul in our presence. Welcome, dear Reader!

Let us embark this day upon a journey into the farthest, darkest reaches of speculative literature.   Herein is a veritable Rogue's Gallery of short stories and articles— some amusing, some informative, some horrifying, some all three at once—which will uproot your preconceived notions about the world we live in.

Within these pages you will touch the depths of Darkness, reach for the stars, ponder mortality and immortality, wonder at our place in the Universe, and marvel at how Good Intentions can go so horribly wrong.

All told, here is a collection to set the mind a-buzz, stir the pot of complacency, and make you look nervously over your shoulder, which is what Speculative Writing is all about. Enjoy!

*****

We all long for peace and harmony in the affairs of the world, and yet, historically, we have long been disappointed. It is a sad truth of human nature that wars and rumors of wars are our daily lot. If only someone would grab the bull by the horns, so to speak, and set this troubled world on the Paths of Righteousness! But the problem with grabbing the bull by the horns, of course, is that said bull can be remarkably unpredictable...

"Best Laid Plans"

June, 1890:

"I should like to know what the *devil* this is about!" was how Lord Edrich greeted Markham, the British Legate there in Charlotte Amalie, capital of the Danish West Indies. The voyage by Royal Navy cutter—there being no ship more appropriate to his station in Bermuda at the moment—was a miserable affair which had his indigestion quite out of sorts. "Well, sir?" he thundered. "What have you to report?"

"I'm afraid I've learnt nothing, m'lord." Markham wilted under Lord Edrich's famously hasty temper. "The Spaniards arrived from Havana two days ago, the Americans arrived yesterday, the French and German delegates just this morning. No one knows anything."

Edrich planted his hefty bulk firmly on the wharf and confronted the smaller man. "Nothing? Nothing, sir? Is this what the Foreign Secretary pays you for?"

"Even the Danish Governor knows nothing, sir!"

"By God, sir! Do you mean to tell me delegates from all the European powers are gathered in this tropic hell, and no one can say why?"

"So it would...ah...a new arrival, m'lord." Markham gestured to a ship just setting into Saint Thomas's tiny harbor.

"Hmmm... Austrian!" Lord Edrich studied the newcomer. "Their new steam frigate, no less. *They're* well out of their allotted place, I daresay."

"She's signaling, sir!" Markham studied the flag hoist on the Austrian's yards. "Have...Russian...and...Italian...on board."

4

"By Jove, *that* must have been a stormy passage!" All three powers had long histories of antagonism toward each other.

"Indeed, sir. One can but wonder at what impelled their governments to agree to such a thing?" Markham was sobered by the thought. "This affair must be of a special order to get *those* lot in one ship."

"Hmmm. Not to mention getting the entire herd of us together on this Godforsaken island." Lord Edrich pondered the 'Special Instruction' he'd received a mere two weeks past from the Foreign Secretary directing him to *'Proceed at once to the Danish West Indies to witness a weapon's test reputed to be of the utmost concern to Her Majesty's government.'* This mystery was taking on sinister undertones if everyone and their dog were to be present. "What is this about a weapon? The Danes are hardly world-beaters, and even if so, why demonstrate it here in the Caribbean?"

"I can't imagine, sir, unless..."

"Unless?"

"...unless...this weapon is so fearful that they prefer to test it here in this remote location?"

"Stuff and nonsense! What can best the power of a proper twelve inch cannon, I ask you?" Lord Edrich sighed in resignation. "I suppose we shall find out soon enough. Well, sir? Where is my carriage?"

"Right this way, m'lord!"

§

Needless to say, with this many official delegates from the world powers present, a formal reception was in order. The Governor of this tiny Danish outpost was a bit overwhelmed, as was the Official Residence, but they managed a modest repast. Finding quarters for them all was more difficult, since there was only one respectable hotel in Charlotte Amalie.

"I am afraid I know nothink of any veapon, *mienheren*," the Governor protested when they ganged up on him at the dinner table. "Vee haff no such demonstration in mind!"

"If not you, then *who?*" the Frenchman demanded.

The Dane spread his hands in frustration. "I haff no idea!" That sorely tried gentleman scarcely got to taste his dinner. The delegates were in a state—predictably so at the thought of a super-weapon—and gave him no peace. His protests did little to calm the storm of curiosity, and he retreated to his quarters as soon as he properly could, leaving them to fume.

The sun set, taking the oppressive heat and humidity of the day with it, and the evening was a pleasant relief as they gathered on the promenade overlooking the harbor.

"Fish has never been my favorite, but it's no more than we can expect from these Danish fellows," Lord Edrich grumbled. The chef's specialty was roasted tuna, which he consumed more than a share of. "At least they can offer a fitting cigar!"

"Indeed, m'lord," Markham mumbled as he stoked his own Havana. "Hello, storms on the horizon!" The French and German were bearing down on them, cleared for action.

Edrich got off the first broadside. "So what have you gentlemen heard of this business?"

"*Aucunement!*" the Frenchman cried. "We have not a clue, nor does the Spaniard. All I know is Le President received a most alarming missive claiming that a dreadful new weapon will be unveiled here, of all places. Why he would take such alarm I cannot say, but take alarm he did."

"It iss zee same mit der Kaiser," the German added. "He received a communique which caused great alarm in court."

"But you have no idea why?"

"*Nichts, mein Herr*...nothing. Vee haff heard nothing as well. Zere must haff been further information in zee message vee vere not privilege to."

For once they were probably telling the truth. "Well, I suppose we shall find out in good time," Edrich grumbled. They spent the next few minutes exchanging chilly pleasantries before drifting off in different directions.

"I have a bit of news, m'lord," Markham said, quietly, when he rejoined the party a few minutes later. "I spread some money about, and have just learnt there is some sort of project under way on one of the minor islands some distance to the Southeast. My informant couldn't learn any details, but there are rumors of ships calling there at night..."

"Ships calling at night? Smugglers, sir!"

"No doubt, but smuggling what?"

"Hmmm... That is the question."

§

The delegates met the next morning on the quay, and their moods were hardly improved. The Danish Governor joined the procession, and was equally out of sorts over a supposed super-weapon being tested in his bailiwick without his knowledge. They spent the time grumbling and arguing among themselves, wondering what this was all about as the sun rose and the day turned warm.

"By God, I hope this isn't some elaborate Fools' Errand!" Lord Edrich complained.

"That would hardly seem wise, m'lord," Markham offered.

"Mocking the British Empire rarely is, to say nothing of all these other people."

They were joined a few minutes later by someone new. "Good morning, gentlemen," he said, somberly.   "I am your host, Professor Marquaid." He was improbably tall and thin, almost emaciated, dressed in an ill-fitting Panama suit. His features were burnt by the tropic sun and his hair was thin and gray, and he had an almost funeral air about him, as if he was the bearer of some tragic news.

"Well if you are, then you may start by explaining what is going on here," Lord Edrich demanded. "I warn you, sir, if this is some sort of Fools' Errand..."

"It is *NOT!*" Marquaid silenced him with a stinging retort. "Everything will be revealed in due course, if you are all up to a brief voyage." He waved at a local fishing vessel tied to the quay, its crew of four natives waiting passively. "Our demonstration site is some distance Southeast of here."

"What? In *that?*" the American objected.

"Unfortunately there are no luxury ocean liners available for hire here in Saint Thomas, so we shall have to make do," Marquaid snapped.   "Your discomfort is a small matter compared to the discomfort your government will feel it they miss out on this demonstration!" His somber mood faded abruptly, replaced by a burning light in his eyes. The abrupt change, and his unexpected assertiveness made them all nervous.

"Now see here, sir! Who the devil are you, and what do you have to do with this?" Lord Edrich couldn't be overawed for long, it seemed. "I should like to see your credentials before I go anywhere."

"The fact that your government took this seriously enough to send you here is all the credentials needed. If you want to defy Downing Street's wishes, do so, but don't waste *my* time!" It seemed this Marquaid was an ill-tempered sort, to be expected of a True Believer. "So, if you *gentlemen* will get aboard, we have a fair trip ahead of us."

There was nothing for it, so they squeezed onto the tiny fishing vessel, which took some doing. The native crew cast loose, and they set out of the harbor. The delegates made themselves as comfortable as they could on the stained decks and endured the overwhelming stench of fish and tar. Marquaid stayed apart from them, standing in the boat's prow watching the sea ahead.

"What do you make of this Marquaid fellow?" Lord Edrich muttered to Markham after they cleared the breakwater.

"I've no idea, sir. I've never heard of him before." He paused to covertly study their host standing aloof in the bows. "The man is a fanatic, sir. If he's devised some sort of super weapon, this could be a problem."

"Indeed." They both watched Marquaid for a time, noting how the native crew, usually a talkative, carefree lot, were subdued, even nervous around their host. "They know something." Edrich gestured furtively at the coxswain.

"The natives always do, sir. Uncanny, that. But my spies have learnt little beyond the bare fact of the project itself."

The sea was picking up a bit once they were clear of land. The fishing boat rode the swells easily, but it was not a comforting journey, made all the worse by the stench of fish and tar, and their nagging worry over what this voyage would reveal. The delegates and the native crew were all silent and withdrawn, as was Marquaid at his station in the bows.

§

Even with a fair wind, it was mid-afternoon when they hove to on the lea of a small island, little more than a sandbar with a few scraggly palm trees and some sawgrass. "Frenchcap Island," Markham said as he consulted a navigation chart. "Uninhabited." The island was about seven hundred feet across, in fact, and an enormous white structure in its center was the only hint of man's presence. As they dropped anchor a few miles off shore, a cutter set out from the island and soon joined them, delivering two more men on board.

"Is it ready?" Markham demanded as they climbed aboard.

"All set," the first one said. "The timer is activated, and you have about five minutes."

"Fine." Marquaid glanced nervously at his watch. "Gentlemen, you will forgive me if I am brief and to the point, since we have but a short time for explanations. My two associates, Professors Van Decamp and Wilson and I are part of an international organization, the World Scientific League, devoted to a systematic approach to scientific discovery. You may know that up to now scientific exploration has been the realm of individuals working on their own with limited resources, often as an adjunct to their teaching duties. Our League has sought to improve on this haphazard process, which has led to some startling, and I daresay disturbing results."

He glanced at his watch again, clearly feeling rushed. "Recently, some of our members made a frightening discovery: a discovery which threatens the very existence of mankind, and poses certain doom for our civilization. We have learned that matter and energy are two different forms of the same thing, like ice and water, and that it is possible to change them back and forth..."

"What is the significance of this?" Lord Edrich demanded. "You're talking of nothing more than ordinary fire!"

"...*except* that fire, combustion, converts but a tiny fraction of the burnt mass to energy. Even the most potent explosives use only a minuscule part of their mass. Our research has found a way to release *all* of the mass as energy!"

"Time," Professor Wilson said as he studied his watch.

Marquaid nodded nervously. "Gentlemen, the moment is upon us. On that island we have prepared a test of this new power, which is set to go off any second now." He grabbed a box and began distributing dark goggles, which his two associates also donned hastily. "For your own safety, you need to wear these, and to turn away from the blast as well."

"You propose to demonstrate a weapon by not permitting us to watch it?" the Frenchman scoffed. "But of course, it is a secret weapon, *no?*"

"Trust me, sir, this is for your own good." Marquaid pressed the goggles into his hand and turned him away, together with the Spaniard. "The flash can blind you otherwise."

"Bunch-a hooey..." the American began, but was cut off when they were enveloped in a blinding glare.

Their first instinct was to turn to see what happened, which those not wearing goggles regretted. The island had been consumed in a vast blinding ball of fire, which rose slowly and majestically on a seething column of smoke until it towered over them, blotting out the afternoon sun. The roar of the explosion reached them moments later: a deafening thunder which rolled and reverberated until it shook them as if they were being beaten. Even as the roar of the blast faded, they were pelted by a hail of fragmented coral, followed in turn by a shock wave which almost capsized their small ship.

It took perhaps five minutes for the calamity to expend its force, and considerably more before they began to recover from the shock. The American was the first to recover his wits. "What...the...hell was *that?*" His exclamation set off a clamor from the delegates which took Professor Marquaid some time to overcome.

"There you have it, gentlemen," he said at last. "That blast was caused by the conversion of *one ounce* of mass by our process. You can see how devastating the result is."

"By...God..." Lord Edrich mumbled. "We were...what...five miles distant?"

"Seven," Marquaid said, grimly. "And that was just a sample."

"You haff sunk our island!" the Danish Governor cried.

10

"*Mien Gott*, zey haff!" The German was equally appalled.

"You can imagine what such a weapon would do if detonated in the heart of a city!" Marquaid said, grimly. "I can assure you militarily useful weapons a hundred times that force are not only possible, but practical!"

"*Mon Deau!* How did you do it?" the Frenchman cried, setting off another clamor.

"You will forgive me if we refuse to tell you," Marquaid managed at last. "The world does not need for this secret to get out!"

"But you must! This is too important to keep from the world!"

"It is too *deadly* to let the world have it, *Monsieur!*"

"It's your *duty* to reveal it to a government who will protect the secret properly!" the American huffed.

"And which government would that be? Which of you will the others all trust? You can see why it is *our* duty to remain silent!"

"It seems to me we can discover the secret soon enough," Lord Edrich growled. "When we get you back to London and turn you over to the tender attentions of Scotland Yard, I daresay you'll talk!"

"*Nein!* Vee vill not allow such a weapon to fall into zee hands of any other power! Zey must come mit us!"

"Never! France must be the guardian of this secret! Anything less is *scandaleux!*"

"We'll get 'em t' talk!" the American vowed.

"You will do no such thing, gentlemen!"

They were all taken aback by Marquaid's sudden assertiveness. Academics simply *did not* address their betters in such a tone. "What do you mean by your impudence, sir?" Edrich demanded.

"I *mean* that the only hope for the human race is to keep such terrible power *out* of the hands of fools such as yourselves!" Marquaid drilled each of them with an icy glare. "*Think* of the consequences of these weapons in the hands of such fatuous children! You would destroy each other; you *know* it's true!"

That produced a chorus of righteous indignation which, nonetheless, failed to move their host. "There is worse news!" he yelled over the clamor, which restored order abruptly.

"These 'atom weapons' are expensive, but a bargain compared to the cost of a modern army," Marquaid went on after a bit. "And the secret, once understood, is something any industrial nation can develop..."

"All the more reason to *make* you talk!" Lord Edrich yelled.

"*That* is the one thing you *will not* do!" Marquaid drilled him with an icy glare. "Understand this, gentlemen: any attempt to force the knowledge of this power from any member of the World Scientific League, and we will release that secret to everyone!"

"You would destroy the world to keep your secret, *Monsieur?*"

"If we must, since the only hope then would be to arm everyone so that no one dare start a war."

"What you propose is appalling, sir!" Edrich cried.

"*You* should talk! The means of modern warfare are hideous enough; if these 'atom weapons' are employed, our civilization will crumble!"

That daunting prospect and the thin fog of steam and coral dust from the former island put a damper on the argument. "What you say is true enough, sir," Lord Edrich said at last. "But can you assure us the secret of these dreadful weapons won't leak out? Scientists are merely human, as patriotic as any. Can you assure us this knowledge won't fall into the wrong hands?"

Marquaid shook his head dolefully. "No, we can't. No one can. As much as we wish this never was developed, and as much as we wish to keep it secret, knowledge is its own truth, and cannot be denied. This is why we prepared this demonstration; not to announce a terrible new weapon, and *certainly* not to sell it to the highest bidder! This demonstration is to convince you all of the threat now hanging like a Sword of Damocles over all our heads. If the secret of this dreadful power can be discovered once, no doubt it will be discovered again. It appears we are doomed...*unless* we chart a bold new direction."

That caught them all off guard. "So what do you propose, *Monsieur?*" the Frenchman asked.

"We must outlaw war!" That produced another round of squawking. "Our one hope is to make war impossible by abolishing all military forces." Marquaid had to shout over the renewed clamor. "In order to insure compliance, we must create a World League with the power to inspect for and punish possible violators. This World League would also maintain an arsenal of these 'atom weapons' for the common defense against rogue nations...great or small."

If his earlier statements produced a storm of indignation, this last unleashed a hurricane. Even the Danish Governor got into the act as they threatened and blustered and vehemently denounced the very idea. Marquaid matched them blow for blow, arguing persuasively that the World League would insure the peace, resolve disputes, improve trade and, ultimately, keep the human race from self-destruction.

It went nowhere. The argument continued well into the evening as they sailed back to Saint Thomas, and even thereafter. It didn't end, in fact, until Marquaid threw up his hands in disgust and stomped off.

§

"By God, that was *quite* a performance!" Professor Van Decamp said when the conspirators could get a moment of privacy at the *vaertshus* where they met frequently for lunch. "I had no idea our creation would make *such* a bang!"

Professor Marquaid greeted his acclaim with a weary chuckle. "Five thousand tons of powdered magnesium and guncotton? I should think so!"

"The biggest photoflash in history! It certainly made an impression on our guests," Professor Wilson added. "Scared the living bejesus out of them!"

"As intended. I think we can expect some interesting results in short order."

"We took a terrible risk, you know." Van Decamp always was the pessimistic one. "Handling so much explosives..." He shook his head in dismay. "If it had misfired, our fraud would have been exposed. We would be ruined."

"The tricky part was getting all those detonators to fire at the same instant, which your electric system solved nicely." Marquaid patted Van Decamp on the shoulder in a reassuring gesture. "You made it work, and because you did, *we* have changed history!"

"Wonderful, I'm sure." Van Decamp sighed in one of his habitual funks. "It's a shame, though. Your fine little speech about a 'World League' was a grand idea. Sad to say, they didn't seem impressed."

Marquaid shorted derisively. "Of course not! The European powers are too caught up in the glory of themselves. The idea of a supra-national body taking away their cherished privilege of waging war upon each other would never work!"

"We can only hope your idea does," Professor Wilson said. "I can't help wondering if they'll really bankrupt themselves?"

"Of course they will! They can't take the chance of another power developing these 'atom weapons', so they'll keep trying to invent the impossible until they ruin themselves. It's human nature; our *real* secret weapon." Marquaid hoisted his coffee cup in a mock toast. "The World Scientific League; serving humanity through flim-flammery! Barnum was right: there's one born every second" That brought on a round of derisive cheer at the success of their gambit.

"I just hope this doesn't trigger a general European war, like we feared," Van Decamp said after a bit.

"*Again*, Van?" Marquaid complained. This was an old argument among them. "Surely they're appalled enough at the thought not to go *that* far!"

Van Decamp sighed. "It would be bloody. I hate the thought of setting off a holocaust on such a scale."

"They aren't *that* stupid," Marquaid said, sternly. "It would be a horror, as our studies predict."

"But suppose they do? What then?"

Marquaid dismissed the unpleasant prospect with the wave of a hand. "They would be too caught up in their own sense of glory to simply make peace despite the obvious stalemate. The fighting would go on until they were devastated, which will serve our purposes just as well."

"God! I hope it doesn't come to that!"

"Either way we will bring the European powers to ruin, thus bringing the Imperial Age to an end. The risk, however terrible, is well worth it."

14

Van Decamp sighed again. "You're right, of course. I just wonder, though..."

"Oh, what *is it*, Van?" Marquaid grumbled. Van Decamp's chronic doubts could be *so* tedious at times.

"...Suppose...it could actually work? Professor Roentgen's discovery of X-rays...do we really know what causes them? Suppose 'atom weapons' could actually be built? What then?"

Marquaid laughed. "Van, you are a dreamer!"

"Quite so," Wilson added. "Still, if such a thing *could* be done, it's better we get this Imperial Age over with before some fool goes and does it."

§

Despite Marquaid's threat, every major and most minor powers tried to get their claws on the conspirators, no doubt intent upon wringing the secret of these terrible weapons out of them. The Danish authorities, themselves eying the secret with deep misgivings since they would be caught in the crossfire of any European war, refused to extradite on the grounds that inventing terrible new weapons was not a crime. Possession is nine points of the law, and for the moment the Danes held the home court advantage. No one liked it (other than the three conspirators), but at least no one considered Denmark a threat.

And so a precarious balance existed for the plotters. They perforce took up residence in Saint Thomas, eeking out a living by teaching in the local schools, and waited for their supposed day of reckoning. The United States threw a scare into them when they proposed to the Danes to buy the islands, which they fancied to rename the U S Virgin Islands, but the Danes saw through this stratagem, and passed.

Time went on. The story of the 'atom weapon' was front page news around the world for a fortnight before abruptly fading from view. The conspirators saw, and greeted the disappearance with solemn pleasure.

Before long, whispers came to them about top scientists vanishing, recruited—forcefully in some cases—by their governments, it was rumored. The conspirators noted and nodded to themselves, knowing what it meant.

Then strange things began happening in world financial matters. Government budgets, traditionally public knowledge, went dark. No one could tell how much was being spent, or for what, other than for non-defense spending which was being slashed to the bone all across Europe. The conspirators observed, and felt a deep sense of satisfaction.

1890 passed into history, followed in due course by the 19th Century. As expected, tensions rose in Europe all the while. The major powers' economies grew shaky, recession set in, the people grumbled at the ever-increasing taxes while the rhetoric grew more inflamed and the borders more tense. The budgets remained deep, dark secrets. More scientists disappeared. War clouds gathered over Europe as diplomatic efforts faltered. The conspirators watched and waited.

Finally it all came unglued over what Otto Von Bismarck described as "Some damn-fool thing in the Balkans."

§

September, 1905

"Have you seen the papers?" Marquaid waved the latest edition of the New York Times—only a week old—which arrived on the inter-island steamer just a short while ago.

"I haven't," Van Decamp said, morosely. "Not that I want to."

"Our predictions were correct," Marquaid went on, remorselessly. "The combination of barbed wire and machine guns has tipped the balance in war so far in favor of defense that forward war has become impossible. They're slaughtering each other, in France and Russia, both."

"If only they'd learnt from the Americans," Van Decamp sighed.

"Who listens to the *Americans?* In any event, their civil war was forty years ago. Out of sight, out of mind with these Europeans, eh?"

"Really, Marquaid, must you gloat over it?"

Professor Wilson turned up just then at the *vaertshus*. "The latest news from Europe came just a while ago." He waved a recent copy of the London Times. "It appears the Germans are falling apart!"

16

Reuters, Paris, September 4, 1905
German forces under Von Holtz are retreating in reported disorder in the direction of Mannheim, pursued by the French under General DuRochelle. The French 1st Army headquarters in Metz described the German move as 'a rout', and state they expect to occupy Saarbrucken within two weeks.

"Hmph!" Marquaid grunted as he reread the passage. "I thought they would last longer."

"They've endured six months of butchery," Van Decamp said. "How any army could take that is beyond understanding."

"Maybe so." Marquaid passed the paper to him. "If it is, it means our plan is working better than anticipated."

"It'll be over sooner, anyway."

"It needed to be done, Van," Marquaid said, gently. "The only way we could end the Imperial Age was to get them to destroy themselves. At least a better world will rise from the ashes."

"You hope."

§

Their hopes in such regard were dashed the next day when the Times made its way over on the mail packet from the Virgin Islands:

Reuters, Paris, September 5, 1905
French Army headquarters in Paris reports they have lost contact with the 1st Army after witnesses here described seeing a 'terrible explosion' in the vicinity of the rapidly advancing front, presently some 165 miles away. Unconfirmed reports state this may signal the use of an 'atom weapon'.

"Oh, dear God!" Wilson muttered as he read it.

"...No...that can't be..." Marquaid mumbled after reading it in turn. "It must have been a conventional mine...explosives."

"Enough explosives that they *saw* the blast in Paris?"

"A munitions bunker, then."

"No one in their right mind would store *that* much explosives in one place!"

"Well it *certainly* couldn't be an 'atom weapon'! Could it?"

"With our luck? Don't count on it," Van Decamp sighed.

§

The next days' Boston Globe confirmed the worst:

Reuters, Berlin, September 5, 1905
German High Command reported the destruction of the French 1st Army, who were lured forward by a feigned German rout onto an 'atom weapon' planted as a mine. The French Army reportedly suffered 150,000 casualties, and is retreating in disorder.

Another item dispelled any lingering doubts:

Reuters, Brussels, September 5, 1905
Scientific authorities at Vrije Universiteit Brussel report evidence of 'radiant-active' dust falling in the region of Brussels, which is believed to have come from the 'atom weapon' recently detonated by the Germans. Unconfirmed reports from Germany suggest the 'atom weapon' used had the destructive power of 1,000,000 tons of gunpowder.

"One...*million*...tons..." Wilson was appalled. "What have we done?"

"They did it!" Marquaid was equally horrified. "Those infernal fools did it! They got the damned things to work!"

"Madame Curie warned us," Van Decamp said, morosely. "She said we shouldn't underestimate the potential of radio-isotopes."

Marquaid rounded on him in anguish. "We're a mathematician, a chemist and a metallurgist, what would we know about 'atom weapons'!"

"This was *your* idea!" Van Decamp cried. "*You* came up with all those formulas! *You* convinced us it was safe! *You* said it'd never work! *You* said they'd bankrupt themselves trying to do the impossible!"

"I...must have made an error," Marquaid mumbled. "Misplaced a decimal...forgot to carry the 'one'..."

"But how *could* they do it?" Wilson asked. "We were *sure* it wouldn't work."

"We *proved* it could be done with our phony demonstration, so they went and *figured out* how!" Van Decamp yelled. "All because of our fraud!"

"Well it's too late for recriminations. What's done is done. The question now is, how do we stop it?"

Marquaid looked bleak. "How *do* we stop Doomsday?"

§

Over the next three months, the Germans detonated two more 'atom weapons', one in the anchorage at Scapa Flow, wrecking much of the Royal Navy, one under an advancing Russian army. The Russians, in turn, detonated two, destroying a German army and the city of Danzig. The British retaliated by sneaking a weapon up the Rhine in a barge and wiping out Dusseldorf, and by smashing the German fleet at Wilhelmshaven. The French destroyed Karlsruhe and Mannheim using unmanned balloons, since no dirigible could hope to survive the blast, which heralded the dawn of strategic bombing. The Italians and Austrians traded destroyed army corps, effectively ending their conflict. Russia and Austria slugged it out with three apiece, with appalling losses. The Japanese—of all people—set one off in Vladivostok, and were promptly repaid by the Russians, ending both countries naval ambitions in the Pacific. Even the Americans detonated an 'atom weapon' in their desert Southwest, apparently to prove they could since they had stayed steadfastly out of 'that European matter'.

By year's end, Europe was looking decidedly moth-eaten. But despite the horrendous destruction and appalling casualties, despite the widespread panic, despite the masses of displaced refugees and the near collapse of their economies, the Imperial powers kept at it, desperate to win at any cost. As Marquaid predicted, they were too caught up in war fever to *think* of compromising with their rivals. The conflict had been propagandized on both sides as a struggle to 'save human civilization'; the 'atom weapons' confirmed everyones' worst overblown fears, turning the struggle into a holy crusade.

The process begun so innocently with barbed wire and machine guns rumbled on in an 'atom weapon' free-for-all until the warring powers teetered on the brink of disintegration.

It had to end eventually, of course. With their streets running in revolution and their armies disintegrating, with food riots growing and their treasuries emptied, the Imperial powers were finally forced to accept the unthinkable. By unspoken consensus, despite the strident demands of their governments, the armies crawled away like wounded animals looking for a place to hole up. The war not so much ended as petered out, leaving Europe a shambles.

§

"Damn!" Marquaid muttered. "We almost had it." The plotters met at the *vaertshus* for lunch to sort out the results of their little scheme a few days after a general armistice was declared. They were half relieved the slaughter was ended and half dismayed that the European powers, though tottering, remained intact.

"It was all for nothing," Van Decamp grumbled.

"So what do we do now?" Wilson asked, plaintively. "We don't dare leave this island, and I, for one, am getting a bit tired of seafood." The rest of the world hadn't forgotten them, and from all accounts they were still *very* wanted men.

"We are *not* going to give up!" Marquaid said, emphatically. "They only need one more push to cause the whole rotten structure to collapse!"

"But how? We're bankrupt, and we don't dare show our faces anywhere."

"The mistake we made was in thinking we could do it all by ourselves." Marquaid spread a copy of the New York Times on the table and pointed out a small financial page item. "All we need is the right leverage!"

*****

We gaze out upon the heavens to the distant, remote stars and galaxies, and our spirits are daunted by the vast distances—distances so great that the numbers are meaningless. To all appearances we are trapped here in our solar system, destined never to touch those distant points of light. But appearances can be deceiving...

"The Light Speed Myth"
From "Astrophysics for Idiots", 5th ed. c. 2118

One of the great misconceptions to come out of 20th century science was the so-called 'light speed barrier'. In this theory, the maximum speed anything can travel in this Universe is the speed of visible light through a vacuum: 299,792,458 m/s. With this came an array of phenomenon born of the convoluted mathematics needed to tie up a host of loose ends: notably the increase in mass and compression of time rate in an object approaching light speed.

This theory was the guiding principle of space exploration (or more precisely the excuses not to waste public moneys on it) until well into the late 21st Century. It is only now that we see the crucial flaw which renders this theory false.

The fundamental mistake made back in the 20th century was simple: speed has to relate to a reference point. The 'speed of light' is relevant only to a 'stationary' observer, and the 'light speed barrier' is only valid if that observer assumes there is a fixed center to the Universe in relation to which all velocities are measured. In fact the Universe is infinite, and thus has no 'absolute' reference point. True, the Big Bang expansion has a center, but this is not the same as a Universal center. Lacking this 'center' reference point, speed becomes solely a matter of the observer's prejudice.

To site the famous example: observer 'A' is 'at rest'. Observer 'B' is traveling at .9 light. Observer 'C' is moving at 1.8 light. 'A' and 'B' can see each other since their relative speed is 'less than light', as can 'B' and 'C'. However, 'A' and 'C' cannot see each other, since each appears to the other to be moving 'faster than light'. However, all three observers are 'at rest' *as far as the Universe is concerned.*

Modern science refers to the measurement of speed, acceleration, vector and related matters as 'Inertial Theory'. In Inertial Theory, there is only one state of mass: at rest. In Universal terms, every mass is at rest, each with its own energy state. So-called 'acceleration' is the process of shifting a mass from one rest state to another by applying energy, while 'velocity' is the apparent energy states of rest mass objects compared to other objects. This relates to Newton's First Law of Motion: "An object at rest will remain at rest unless acted upon by an outside force."

Inertial Theory has three characteristics which translate the four-dimensional space-time Universe into a three-dimensional phenomenon: the 'energy/inertia ratio', 'time', and 'vector'. The 'energy/inertia ratio' is an expression of the energy imparted to an object, multiplied by 'time', affecting how efficient the ratio is in shifting the mass, compared to its 'inertia'. 'Vector' expresses a 'polarization' of the 'energy/inertia ratio' on the object in the four-D Universe. In practical terms, the greater the 'energy x time/inertia' ($V=ExT/I$), the more 'vector' is applied.

Apparent 'motion' is an illusion created by comparing various four-dimensional rest-state masses from a three-dimensional viewpoint. Since we cannot perceive time as a dimension, in our limited viewpoint 'vector' translates into a three-dimensional direction, while 'time' translates into the duration of energy input, thus velocity. The ETIV (energy x time/inertia=vector) thus accumulated has a polarization which can affect other ETIV masses. If the ETIV polarization of two masses becomes aligned, they can be drawn into each other—what we in our three-dimensional perspective call a 'collision'. Conversely, EITV polarization can repel objects, causing them to move away from each other in three dimensions. ETIV polarization produces the whole world of motion phenomenon we take for granted.

While the theorists of the 20th Century failed to grasp this, they did skirt around it in trying to explain a host of associated phenomenon. The most critical of these is the apparent increase in an object's mass and the contraction of its time rate as it approaches the perceived 'speed of light'. This comes from the inherent conflict in the 'energy/inertia' ratio.

'Energy' is an active state seeking to affect the rest mass, while 'inertia' harkens back to Newton's First Law. These two are fundamentally incompatible. In order for 'energy' to overcome 'inertia', 'energy' must counterbalance 'inertia', with the excess creating 'vector'; the greater this counterbalance, the 'energy/inertia' ratio, the more 'vector' is imparted.

Where this gets sticky is that as the 'vector' increases, so does the amount of excess 'energy', which is absorbed into the mass. As Einstein stated in his famous E=MC2, energy and mass are equivalent and transmutable. As the energy is absorbed, it translates into greater mass. Thus the 'energy' applied must increase as 'vector' does. At the perceived 'speed of light', the mass becomes infinite, thus no further 'vector' can be created. The apparent 'time' compression is a result of the massive imbalance of the other three dimensions.

What finally brought the 'speed of light' crashing down was the invention of the mass polarizer. Scientists trying to revitalize the space program in the late 21st Century realized they could never accomplish anything until they could solve the tremendous energy cost of boosting cargos into orbit.

What they found was a means of reorienting the rest mass 'inertia' so it no longer opposed the input of 'energy'; in effect polarizing it out of phase. The result, effectively, was to reduce the 'inertia' of an orbital shuttle by some ninety percent, thus vastly improving its 'energy/inertia ratio' and resulting payload.

While the original intention was to reduce the energy cost of building the orbital solar power collectors, it wasn't long before the idea was applied to interstellar travel. It was discovered that if enough power is poured into a mass polarizer, a starship's inertia can be effectively reduced to zero: thus bypassing the 'energy/ inertia ratio', its resulting mass buildup, and the light speed barrier. Once these have been bypassed, there is no effective limit to how fast a starship can go.

Where this new-found freedom will take us, no one knows.

*****

We like to think we act with the best of intentions, but all too often life gets in the way, and we wake up one morning to discover that what truly matters has passed us by. The saddest part is coming to this realization on the morning when we don't wake up...

"A Birthday Gift"

Spring was well along, although the last of the winter snow still lay in odd corners on the muddy playground. The first grass of spring was starting to push up, a faint tint of bright green on the bare earth. The air was brisk, and the sky was a beautiful, surreal blue, with golden sunlight playing on clouds like fluffy white sheep as they drifted past. It was a perfect day such as one rarely sees in life; like a promise that somehow all was right with the world.

Mrs. Kemmelmann, the Assistant Principal, stood by the office window enjoying a break and admiring the lovely scene outside. The school year would be over soon, and they would all face a summer of making do or making out with odd summer jobs. This late in the school year was always a trying time. The children were restless, eager for the year to end, while the staff pondered the future with resignation or misgivings. She sighed, and shook off those negative thoughts. Tomorrow would come soon enough. For the moment, there was the bright mid-day sun, and the first sprouting grass, and the fluffy clouds, and all was right with the world.

Her reverie was broken when she saw the old man tottering up the walk toward the main entrance. He was dark complected, his thin crown of snowy white hair accenting his black face. He must have been burly once, but now was a shrunken scarecrow. His clothes hung loosely on his frame, and he walked with a weary shuffle as if life itself was too great a burden.

She pondered him with a faint sense of unease. The world being what it is these days, adults are not encouraged to loiter on school grounds, although he seemed too old and feeble to be up to anything alarming. Nonetheless, he was an intruder where adults

24

are viewed with suspicion, so she moved to intercept him at the main entrance.

"Can I help you?" she asked when he arrived.

He didn't answer for a moment, as he had to gasp for breath as if his shuffling walk winded him. "I can only stay for a moment," he said at last in a thin, wispy voice. "I have to leave, but I couldn't go without giving my granddaughter her birthday present." He held up a brightly wrapped package. "Kayla Washington, seven years old today. I understand she's in a Mrs. Jensen's class; could you please show me the way?"

"I'm sorry. School policy..."

"Please," he implored her. "I don't have much time. I'll only be a minute. For her?"

"Well..." She hesitated at the sight of his waxy features and trembling hands. He didn't look well at all, in fact. "Are you all right?" she asked. "If you're sick..."

"I'm just old, is all. A man only lives for so long, you know." He give her a solemn, pleading look. "What troubles me isn't contagious."

He was a tragic figure; it was too much for her to deny his simple request. "Well, I guess for a moment." She glanced at her watch. "They're at lunch right now. If you'll follow me?"

She led him down the hall, his shambling footsteps echoing faintly in the emptiness. She held back to match his tottering pace, and wondered what would drive someone in his obvious condition to such an effort. He struggled along doggedly despite his weakness as if he knew he needed to get this done quickly.

"Do you need to rest?" she asked when he faltered half way down the hall.

He waved her off. "No...thank you. I'm just old, is all. It happens to the best of us." He fondled the bright paper box with a faraway look in his eyes. "We just get old..."

He was silent for a bit, breathing deeply as he recovered his strength. "It used to be I'd walk for miles a day, climb up and down scaffolding, lug survey equipment..." He sighed in resignation. "Where did the years go?"

"Look, maybe you should sit down for a few minutes."

He held up a hand. "I've sat long enough. I've waited too many minutes." He offered her a gentle smile. "I only have one more walk to make and then I'll be done." He glanced at the hall clock and straightened up with an effort. "I'd say lunch is nearly over. We need to get a move-on."

Lunch time *was* nearly over. The crowd of grade-schoolers was thinning out as they drifted out onto the playground, leaving the cafeteria an emptiness filled with faint echos. They finally found a little girl sitting alone at a table methodically peeling and eating an orange. She was neatly dressed in a too-large sweater and coveralls, her hair was done in tidy pigtails, and she wore an ornate beaded necklace.

The old man stopped a few paces from her and smiled gently as he watched. "Kayla?"

She looked up at him in surprise. *"Grampa?"* Then with a delighted squeal of "GRAMPA!" she hurled herself into his arms, almost knocking him off his feet.

"Hello Lil' Flutterby!" He managed to corral the excited seven year old in one arm as he settled onto a convenient chair. "Today's your birthday!"

"Grampa!" She hugged him with childish enthusiasm, causing him to wince, but the light of joy in his features transformed him, seeming to fill him with new life. Finally he was able to peel her off, and showed her the box he carried.

"You're seven years old today, my lil' sweet Flutterby. I brought you something to celebrate."

She studied the package for a moment like she was confused, then tore the paper off. Inside was a colorful box from a craft supply house; a box full of sea shells. "I know how much you love to make your necklaces," he said, tenderly. "So I got these for you."

She pried open the lid and examined the shells; round and fan-shaped, a rainbow of colors and sizes. "Oooohhh! They're pretty! Thank you, Grampa!"

"Happy birthday, Lil' Flutterby."

Then she stopped admiring her new gift, and turned to look at him solemnly. "Grampa, did you get better?"

26

He hesitated for just a moment, then smiled. "No, darling, but I'm all right now. The pain is gone."

"But...momma said you'd..."

"Yes, dear. The angels have come to take me away. They come for all of us eventually, but I couldn't miss your birthday, could I? They said we could stop by to give you your present."

She was silent for a long moment as she seemed to shrink into herself. Finally she said, "Good bye, Grampa," softly. Then she clutched her box of sea shells to her chest and wandered back to the lunch table.

As soon as she was out of earshot, Mrs. Kemmelmann turned on him. "*That* was *inexcusable!*" she hissed. "How could you *say* that to a child? What kind of man are you?"

"A dead one." His tone was so empty, so matter of fact that it stopped her cold. "And I only told her the truth. She knew this was coming; she'll get over it."

"But..."

"A man makes mistakes in his life," he said, quietly. "A man gets so focussed on the prize that he loses track of what really matters." He glanced at Kayla and sighed. "I was never there for her father when he was young. Always busy, always out there hustling, building highways and bridges, making a big name and big money."

He struggled to his feet with an effort. The light of joy which suffused him earlier had faded, replaced by solemn satisfaction, and regret. He watched Kayla for a moment, and shook his head sadly. "Being a black man in a white man's profession, I felt I had to hustle, to be more efficient, more dedicated, more on-the-job than the next guy. Anything to get noticed, anything to be more competitive. Anything to excel, to be the best civil engineer of them all. I never realized until it was too late what a fool I was. I lost my wife and son because of it, lost out on being a husband and father. Kayla...gave me a chance to set it to rights." He faltered, staring at nothing in dejection. "One last chance," he mumbled.

A group of children came running past, all noise and commotion and youthful energy; a stark contrast to his solemn weariness.

"You see...I've been in a nursing home for the last several months...unconscious...on life support. I died a few minutes ago, but I couldn't go without giving her a birthday gift. She loves to make her necklaces, so it seemed like a perfect choice." He smiled as he glanced at Kayla, and a tear ran down his withered cheek. "The Good Lord...well...sometimes a man's prayers are answered."

She stared at him, appalled, and saw clearly how he must be...have been...at death's door. And in some shaken, bewildered corner of her mind, she knew what he said was all true. Every word of it. Her first instinct, as always, was for the children, and she turned to look at Kayla sitting at the lunch table fiddling with her sea shells, tears rolling down her cheeks.

"She's a smart child. Talented. It wouldn't surprise me if her artistic instinct really came to something some day."

She turned back to look at him, but he was gone.

*****

It is said that great men, truly successful men, are driven by their inner demons to reach above what mere mortals might achieve. Success has its price, of course. The demons which goad us forth can also be our undoing if one's outlet for that drive is suddenly taken away...

"The Game's Afoot"

"So, Holmes, you have finally frustrated me." Doctor Moriarty was facing his calamity coolly enough. "But I daresay you are frustrated now as well! Simple justice, don't you agree?"

This would be a day long remembered on the streets and in the tabloids and the police blotters of Great Britain. Sherlock Holmes had finally triumphed over his arch-nemesis, the infamous master criminal, Doctor Moriarty!

"I would have thought you better than to make hollow taunts, Doctor," Holmes replied, coldly. He savored the moment in his own aloof way, drinking in the thrill of victory as if it were as palpable as the London fog which shrouded them. "Your own cupidity led you to this, and you might have the good form to acknowledge it."

"Indeed, I do, sir!" Moriarty tugged vainly against the cuffs with which Inspector Lestrade had just securing his wrists. "You laid a cunning trap and I, to my lasting chagrin, fell into it! Well fought, I say." He returned Holmes' chilly gaze without quarter. For all their honeyed eloquence, they were bitter enemies who stood at the end of a long and arduous battle.

Holmes greeted this admission with a frosty smile. "Then you will forgive me if I do not share your view of the moment, considering you are the only one wearing that particular jewelry." He gestured to the heavy iron cuffs. "Just as I am sure you will understand if I do not seem frustrated by this turn of events. We have, as you say sir, simple justice indeed!"

The police wagon was arriving, so Holmes contented himself with that final jibe. It had been a long day going into a late night, and the endless drizzle weighed them all down. But as tired and chilled as he was, he felt light-hearted. Justice it was, indeed. Not so simple, perhaps; a long, dogged pursuit with many twists and setbacks, but certainly final. He drew rare and profound satisfaction from the moment, permitting himself a small sense of arrogant pride as he and Doctor Watson turned to go.

"And now that I am gone, who will test you, Holmes?" Moriarty called after him.

"Eh?" Holmes came up short and spun on his heel. That comment dashed his smugness and sent a peculiar chill down his spine. "What do you mean, sir?"

Moriarty regarded him silently, calmly, as if he held some unexpected trump card even at this, his stroke of midnight. For a fleeting instant, Holmes feared Moriarty would take the answer with him to the grave...

"What I mean, sir," Moriarty said grimly, "is that the Barbarian in you will not rest with my demise, and there is no one else worthy to take my place."

"Barbarian?" Holmes scoffed, archly, "Really, Doctor! What rubbish from a learnéd man such as you!"

"Oh, but you are a Barbarian, Holmes, just as I!" Moriarty's eyes lit up with excitement. "We are Barbarians of the mind! Of the will! Are we not every bit as ruthless and independent and set by our own standards as the Viking marauders of a thousand years ago?" He cast a contemptuous look at Inspector Lestrade and the two London bobbies. "We are not sheep. We cannot run with the herd. We are the wolves of our time—just as the Vikings in their day!—and like wolves, we must have our hunt! Our prey!"

He straightened his shoulders, took a deep breath, and looked Holmes squarely in the eye. "And like wolves, no mere sheep can give us the battle we crave. So I ask you again, sir, now that you have beaten me, who will test you?"

Holmes locked eyes with him for a long moment as Lestrade and Doctor Watson huffed in proper British indignation. Frozen seconds passed between them, and Holmes suddenly realized he was breathing hard. "You are mad," he said at last, shakily.

Doctor Moriarty offered a crooked smile, a smile which said he had won. "That may be. But if so, it is far more wondrous than this pallid imitation you call sanity."

Inspector Lestrade had enough by then, and grasped Moriarty's arm. "Come along with this lunatic raving, you."

But Moriarty shrugged him off and added, "I think, rather, it is that we are damned, Holmes."

Holmes raised an eyebrow. "Damned, sir? How?"

"We do not belong in this time! We are meant for a different age, an age not smothered in rules and proprieties. There is no place in this tepid world for the likes of us. As I say, Holmes, we are damned, you and I."

For a long moment their eyes locked again and it was Holmes who finally turned away, giving Doctor Moriarty one last tiny triumph. As the Inspector took Moriarty in hand, Holmes stared off into the gloomy night, his heart troubled, unable to behold his final triumph.

"One last thing, Holmes, before we part." Moriarty seemed calmer now, almost rational again. "A small gift for you, something I have held for a long time." He gestured with his chin toward his vest. "There in my pocket."

Reluctantly, Holmes explored his vest pocket, extracting a fine chain with a small silver pendant. He held it up to the dim light of the street lamp and examined it closely. "A Thor's Hammer," he concluded at last. "An original, from the look of it."

"And honestly gained, I can assure you." Moriarty smiled sheepishly as if the thought were an embarrassment. "I found it in a pawn shop in Scotland when I was but a lad. It struck my fancy, and I have had it ever since. I suppose you might call it a good luck charm."

"Indeed?" Holmes fingered the pendant uncertainly. "But why would you give it to me?"

Moriarty shrugged. "I suppose...you might call it a token of the bond between us, of what we are. You have finally proven yourself the Master, and it seems only appropriate that it go to you. Certainly I shan't be needing it any longer." Their eyes met again, and Holmes could see a queer sense of...resignation? Completion? No, it was a sense of finality, a sense that Moriarty had come to a destination long expected and long desired. They both knew he would go to the gallows for his multitude of sins.

For once in his life, Sherlock Holmes was bemused as the Constables lead his now-fallen nemesis away. The pendant dangled forgotten from his hand as he tried to recapture the thrill of the moment, without success.

§

The dreary English winter gave way to a dank English spring when an article on the third page of the London Times reported that the infamous Doctor Moriarty had finally gone through the Hangman's Gate.

Holmes read the article morbidly, then his head sank listlessly against the back of his chair as the paper slid off onto the floor. Since their last encounter, he had felt a profound sense of gloom— of loss, he realized when he analyzed it. For all that he despised Doctor Moriarty, now that he was gone, Holmes felt an emptiness no other antagonist could fill.

There had been a few significant cases since, and the old spirit of the chase had risen in him again as he confronted these would-be challengers. But it had all been too brief, too perfunctory. Ruthless and cunning though they were, they proved no match for him: serving only to remind him of the one challenger now forever beyond his reach.

And so he brooded, slouching in his easy chair before the fire until even the familiar confines of 221B Baker street became a prison. His friends became worried for him, and then alarmed. Doctor Watson frequently badgered him to try to cajole him out of his funk, as he was doing just now.

"All this moping about isn't good for you, 'olmes." His strained bonhomie was almost worse than the disease. "There are plenty of cases crying for your attention at the 'Yard. I'm sure Inspector Lestrade would appreciate your help."

"The good Inspector can manage without me, I am sure."

"But Inspector Lestrade..."

"For God's sake, Watson, leave off!" In an agony of frustration, Holmes stormed out of the flat as his friend stared after him in dismay.

He walked aimlessly for the longest time, lost in the twisting alleys of fog-shrouded London, and lost in his own black

32

melancholy as well. *'Who will test you now?'* Moriarty asked. Who indeed? Oh, there were the usual murderers and bank swindlers, but they were nothing—mere shovel work to pay the rent. Why, by God, without Moriarty, he was no better than a Pinkerton man!

That appalling thought rooted him to the spot on some nameless street corner, his chest suddenly aching with unaccustomed fear. Dreading the worst, he clutched at his heart...and felt something hard pressed beneath his fingers. Without thinking, he dug in his vest pocket, and came up with the Thor's Hammer.

'There is no place in this world for the likes of us,' Moriarty's words echoed in his mind as it glittered in the dim light of a street lamp. *'We are damned, you and I.'* Holmes could see it was true. And like the damned, he was beyond all mortal ken, for life itself was meaningless.

The truth was there before him, had been all along, and now he was forced to confront it. What did he care for London, whose dank, depressing soot and smoke and fog clung to him like a funeral shroud? What did he care—and his legendary gifts of perception and analysis forced him to admit it—what did he care for Britain? Or the law? Or any of it? What were they to him? Mere ants, mortals of lesser clay who trudged through their blind existence with no hint of their own insignificance.

Appalled at where his own remorseless reasoning had taken him, he asked himself, *'What do I care about, if anything?'*

The chase, of course. Moriarty had been a fitting adversary in a relentless battle of wits which tested his—their!—measure to the fullest. Together they rose to epic heights of battle, far above mere crime and detection. Their struggle was a battle of Titans!

He gasped for breath as his heart raced, his pulse pounding in his ears like drums. War drums! He clutched the Thor's Hammer to his chest as the icy thrill run down his spine once again—the fever-fire—the raw blood passion of battle. He could understand now why Moriarty went mad—and he must have *been* mad to have felt such passion! And he knew he was in the grip of that madness as well. Just as Moriarty said, he was truly a Barbarian.

"There you are 'olmes!" It was Watson, coming up the street all in a huff with a London bobby in tow. "We've been looking all over for you!"

The last Barbarian in merry old England. Just as suddenly as it came, the fever-fire left him, dashing his spirit into the miserable clinging chill of the London night. Doctor Moriarty was hanged. Their battle was ended forever. Who, indeed, would test him now, he wondered? There was no one. The future stretched before him; dank, chill, empty of all purpose; a future unbearable; a life without meaning.

His soul recoiled at the thought, and he sought desperately for some escape, some idea, some worthy foe. But how could any one man...then he paused as revelation came to him...why did it have to be one man? Why couldn't his adversary be more than one? But what combination of foes could give him worthy battle as Doctor Moriarty had?

"Eliminate all other possibilities," he mumbled to himself as he struggled desperately against his rising tide of despair. "And whatever remains...however unlikely...must be...the truth." That cardinal principle helped him solve his most baffling cases, and now he applied it remorselessly to the greatest mystery of his career.

"Eh? What did you say, 'olmes?" Watson was beside himself with worry. "'Ere, you've gone out without your coat! Come in before you catch your death of cold!"

And then he knew the answer. It was an appalling answer: one which startled him like he had never been startled before, an answer only his profound gifts of perception and analysis could conceive—nay!—could allow him to accept!

"'olmes?"

But how could he... *Could* he?

"'olmes?"

There was no choice. Moriarty was right: he was damned. He had to have his hunt, his prey. He must have the challenge as the opium smoker must have his nepenthe. Without it he was doomed to a living death.

"'Ere now, 'olmes. What's with you?"

34

It would not be easy. But if it were, why would he bother? Surely Doctor Watson could never know! His eyes flicked back and forth, unseeing, his heart beat faster and his pulse began pounding in his ears again. Indeed, conducting himself right under the nose of his faithful associate would make the challenge all the greater! More! To recruit no less than Inspector Lestrade and the legendary Scotland Yard as his unwitting accomplices!

"Are you all right 'olmes?" Watson was puzzled and worried by his continued silence.

The fever-fire burned within him, dispelling the dank London fog and the dank gloom in his soul. His pulse pounded, his nerves tingled with the thrill of pending battle This had to be! There was no other course for the last Barbarian in merry old England!

On a nearby stoop lay a tattered remnant of the day's London Times, a clearly visible headline reading:

"Crown Jewels Exhibition In Paris."

Moriarty was right: he was damned. He understood his old nemesis now, and pitied him. Sherlock Holmes relaxed his grip on the Thor's Hammer and slipped it into his vest pocket. "Watson," he said simply, unmoving, "The game's afoot."

*****

We rely, as a people, on law enforcement to protect us from the predators in our own ranks. The comforting presence of the cop on the beat assures us that wrong done unto us will be set right. But the Long Arm Of The Law has a finite reach which most of us may not realize...

"Miss Jane Marckell"

Miss Jane Marckell, middle-aged librarian from Cincinnati, Ohio, vanished on her way to work one rainy September morning. That worried her coworkers, since she hadn't missed a day in twelve years. By late afternoon, after calling her home repeatedly, they were frantic. Finally they called the police, who found her purse the next day—ransacked and soaked in blood—in an alley a few blocks from the library.

Now the cops were worried. The purse went to the crime lab, who confirmed that the blood was hers and lifted a host of fingerprints. Now they had a name, John Reims, and a reference to Vancouver, Washington. Vancouver had indeed heard of him, and were glad to be rid of him. They sent their condolences and all the info they had. By then, everyone was worried.

'Vancouver Johnny' was a sick bastard with a rap sheet as thick as a phone book. Drugs, mostly, and no end of petty crimes to support his habit. He was busted more than once for pushing, and did both local and state time, but he was a clever sumbitch who managed to outwit the law more often than not. He degenerated over time into smash-and-grab, muggings, armed robbery, and random violence. The one time they did have a solid beef on him, the case fell apart when the star witness disappeared, leaving lots of blood, but no body. The violence got worse as his mental state deteriorated under a devil's brew of street drugs, climaxing in a botched home invasion which produced a lot more blood. Sloppy police work and a sharp lawyer got him out on bail a few months back, and he vanished—only to turn up in Cincinnati.

The Cincinnati cops turned out to roust the street, and they soon hit paydirt. 'Vancouver Johnny' was new in town, but he already had a rep; the street people eagerly put aside their fear of the law long enough to finger him. His crash was a piece of ratty plywood propped up on some stolen cinder blocks between a railroad embankment and a dumpster in a bad part of town. There they found some of her clothes, her library card, and a lot more blood.   They staked the place out, and 'Vancouver Johnny' stumbled into their arms a few hours later.

§

"Where is she?" Detective Bart Franklin demanded for the umpteenth time. "Give her up. Make this easier on yourself."

'Vancouver Johnny' was tall and emaciated, deeply burned by the sun and wind, with strangler's hands, scraggly hair, and a two week stench. He sat handcuffed in a metal chair in one of the interrogation rooms while Franklin and Detective Joe Horton tag-teamed him. Most suspects would cave under those two, but he just gave them his twitchy, wild-eyed smile.

"Naw, man. She my ol' lady. Found me a good woman t' keep me goin'."

Horton jumped at him from off side. "Is she still alive?"

"If she is, you can help yourself," Franklin added.

"Cut your losses, Reims! Where is she?"

Reims' face split with that freakish grin. "She's fine. She my ol' lady. She all mine, f'ever 'n ever." They were getting heartily sick of his expression.

Homicide dealt with the scum of humanity, and they were hardened veterans of the street wars, but *this* guy...there was something about his aimless wide-eyed stare and that twitchy smile which gave them the shivers. Franklin could see why Washington State had such a hard time with him.   Those crazy eyes...like something out of a nightmare. That look stayed in some terrified corner of the mind. No one would want to meet those eyes in a dark alley. Small wonder they had few witnesses, and fewer who were willing to testify.

"Come off it, Reims!" Franklin was losing his cool under his relentless, aimless smile. "She wouldn't have anything to do with the likes of you. Do the right thing and give her up."

"Naw, man, you can't have her. She my ol' lady. I'll take care of her f' now on. You'll see."

Despite his assurances, or because of them, neither detective held out much hope for her.

§

He went to trial in due order, and despite not having a body, there was plenty to convict him on. The jury took one good look at him, turned up their noses, and voted the death penalty. That was about as expected, and Cincinnati breathed a sigh of relief (as did Vancouver, Wash). Then some hotshot anti-death penalty lawyer got involved, and started arguing the case right up the ladder. That was about as expected, too.

The years went by as the case dragged on through the State courts and up to the Federal courts. The sad fate of Miss Marckell soon faded from view except for an occasional news item in the back pages, and even that ended after a while. They kept looking for her body for a long time, but the urgency faded, and eventually her corpse was filed under 'unfinished business'. Life went on.

Then 'Vancouver Johnny' changed his game. He abandoned the cheap suit they gave him, let his hair and beard grow out, and began arguing that he was guilty, and should get the needle.

"Have you no remorse for the victim?" Harris, the assistant DA, asked.

Reims lolled on the witness stand in studied contempt. "Naw, man. Found me a good woman. She'll keep me comp'ny once I check out-a here."

Harris hesitated. That didn't make sense. "You don't really think you'll walk the street again, do you?"

"Don' need to, man. I'll see her in the sweet bye and bye, right after I check out."

By now Harris was confused by Reims' endless non-sequitur, as were so many before him. "You've been given the death penalty. So you figure to get parole?"

Reims hunched forward in his seat and gave him an evil glare. "Man, you turn me loose, I'll kill someone. You put me in jail, I'll kill someone." He gave the judge a chilling look as only he could. "The only way you rid of me is the needle!"

The lawyers argued he was insane, and didn't know what he did. He stated emphatically that he did know, and would do it again given the chance. The lawyers argued he was incapable of helping his defense. He said he had no intention of doing so. The lawyers argued he was suicidal, and should be declared insane. He insisted he never wanted them in the first place, and fired them loudly and repeatedly in court. The lawyers argued they should be allowed to proceed with his defense whether he wanted their help or not. The appeal was put on hold while they argued *that* one up the ladder.

The one positive thing to come out of all this was the story got some brief national attention.

§

"I've been following the Marckell case, and I think I may be able to help you." Doctor Edwards was portly and balding, dressed in a tweed jacket with elbow patches, and looked for all the world like a college professor. He showed up on a rainy afternoon about a week after the case was put on hold to confront the Homicide team.

Lieutenant Franklin, now head of Homicide, considered him doubtfully. "How?"

"I believe it may be possible to connect with the victim's spirit."

Franklin was already having a bad day brooding over the Marckell case, and that ticked him off. "One thing we don't need around here is another damned palm-reading psychic!"

"I am *not* a psychic," Edwards said, stiffly. "I am a psychic *phenomenon* researcher." He pulled his wallet out, and handed the Lieutenant his card.

"Psychic researcher, eh? What's the difference?" Franklin checked out the card. "CalTech? What is CalTech doing with fortune telling?" He eyed Edwards suspiciously. "You designing some kind of high-tech ouija board for the Pentagon?"

Edwards was annoyed, but kept his cool. "You might say that. We are researching psychic phenomenon to develop telepathy for...certain applications. We stumbled onto some interesting facts which may apply to this case."

"Oh?" Franklin glanced doubtfully at Detective Sergeant Horton. "What sort of facts?"

"We discovered the consciousness, the human identity, the soul if you will, is symbiotic to the physical body. This consciousness can continue after death for an indeterminate length of time."

"No kidding?"

"Fine," Horton grunted. "So what does this mean to us?"

"I understand the body is still missing. If you have it, would it improve your case?"

"Damn right it would!" Franklin said. This was major-league off the wall, but they were eager to grab *anything* which could help find her remains.

"If the victim's consciousness is still active, she may know where the body is buried."

§

That was about the wildest thing any of them ever heard, but Franklin had brooded over Miss Marckell's case for most of his career, and the chill autumn rain—the same sort of drizzling rain he remembered from the day they found her purse—made it all too visceral. It took some persuading, but he finally decided to give the good doctor his chance.

Edwards got on the phone and called his lab at CalTech, which started a shit storm reaching all the way to Washington DC. It seems the doctor's research was you-better-believe-it secret: the Pentagon went into hysterics and the CIA had kittens. He kept at it, pointing out that the soul sensor project had nothing to do with the 'certain applications' they were working on...that these were the *cops*, fer Christ's sake...that here was a chance to test their theories in the field...blah, blah, blah...

It went nowhere. Franklin was still skeptical after all this, but the fate of Miss Marckell had haunted him for years, and the rain was still falling when he left the precinct. He stood in the parking lot looking up at the gray sky...and instead of heading home, he went to the local Senator, a hard case law-and-order man who packed serious weight on the Judiciary Committee.

Edwards' wild tale took some selling, but the Senator owed a few favors, so *he* kicked it upstairs. A week later, two surly FBI agents arrived in Cincinnati, by Presidential order, with the doctor's gismo, which turned out to be a gray metal box the size of a large suitcase whose only features were a speaker grille, some knobs and dials, and a jack for a microphone.

They gathered in Franklin's office for the big experiment, and a stellar cast it was. Doug Harris, newly appointed as the DA, was there, as was Horton and Doctor Albert, the police psychologist. On a last minute thought, they included Reverend Clay, Miss Marckell's former priest, on the off chance she might need his help. The two FBI agents loomed ominously in the background. They dug through the evidence cage, and came up with the plastic box with her purse and oddments of clothing recovered from Reims' crash. They were stiff with long-dried blood, so they left them in the container while Edwards fitted a pair of probes into the mess.

"Okay, Doctor," Franklin grumbled when Edwards got through fiddling with the thing. "Let's get it done."

Edwards flipped a switch. A light glowed, a needle moved, and he nodded to Franklin. Franklin hesitated, then took a deep breath and picked up the microphone. "Hello? Miss Marckell? Can you hear me?"

"What?" The voice from the speaker was definitely a middle aged woman, disoriented and tinged with panic. "Who's there? Who are you?"

"Miss Marckell, I'm Lieutenant Franklin, of the police..."

"Oh, thank *God!* You have to catch him! He's a *beast!*"

"Miss Marckell..."

"He's a mad animal! He'll kill someone else..."

"We have him, Miss Marckell. He'll never hurt anyone again."

There was a moment's silence, then, "*Ohhhh, thank GOD!*"

"Miss Marckell, do you know what happened to you?"

There was a painful silence, and she finally said, "Yes. H-he killed me."

"I'm sincerely sorry, Miss Marckell. The trial is going on now, and he'll get the needle for sure."

"Good," with a tinge of hurt righteousness.

"But now we need to take care of you. We still haven't recovered your body. Can you tell us where it is?"

There was another painful silence. "...no. I...don't know where it is. I don't even know where I am."

41

They exchanged confused looks. "Can you describe where you are?"

"It's...black. It's blank; empty. There's nothing."

§

"Okay, you convinced me," Franklin said. This went way beyond off-the-wall, but none of them could see how Edwards could rig the test or what he would gain from it. "Now what about this void she's in?"

Doctor Edwards was vexed. "I have no idea. Her soul should be free after the body's death."

"Limbo," Reverend Clay muttered, which focussed them on him. "She's in limbo, trapped with her body."

"So what about Heaven and all that?" Horton demanded.

Clay pondered anxiously for a long moment. "It's... Last Rites!" His eyes lit up with Revelation. "It's something found in every religion—a ritual to speed the soul to the afterlife. Without it...she's trapped."

"A ghost?"

Clay paled. "Yes. That would explain the whole ghost phenomenon...souls which never received Last Rites...were never freed from their bodies."

Franklin shot a hard look at Doctor Edwards. "That right, doc?"

"It makes sense," Edwards muttered. "The soul and body are bonded symbiotically. They may need an external force to separate them. Last Rites *could* be some sort of psychological key to unlock the bond."

"It could also explain about having your soul stolen by the Devil," Doctor Albert said.

"Come off it!" Horton snapped. "You don't really buy that bit about the Devil?"

"I...don't know," Clay mumbled. "I always assumed there was, but in light of this discovery..." He faltered, thinking hard.

Doctor Albert ran with it. "It *could* be a manifestation of our fear of death. The soul, and soul stealers, are found in every religion. It could be the tradition of Last Rites started as an instinctive defense against death."

42

"Or it could be the soul exerting a subconscious influence to insure its self preservation," Doctor Edwards added.

"But she received Last Rites, from you," Horton accused Reverend Clay. He and several of the Homicide Squad attended her funeral. "So what went wrong?"

"I..." Clay faltered in confusion again. "She... We didn't have the body. We...may need the body to make the Last Rites work."

§

They growled at each other for a while, and decided the only thing to do was trek up to the state prison to debate psychic phenomenon with a murderous psychopath.

Reims sat on the floor of his cell when they arrived, in lotus position, eyes closed, rocking gently back and forth. He was singing softly to himself, something which sounded like a snatch of an old camp revival tune.

"Gonna die in the sweet bye-and-bye."

"Gonna fly in the sweet bye-and-bye."

"Gonna die in the sweet bye-and-bye."

"Gonna fly in the sweet bye-and-bye."

"Will you put a sock in it?" the duty sergeant grumbled.

Reims twitched like he'd been nodding off. He broke off his hymn, looked around in confusion for a moment, then gave him that twitchy smile. "Nuh-uh. 's my religious rights. Got to sing me a song, sing me free after I go." He ignored the Sergeant's peeved look, and went back to singing.

"Gonna die in the sweet bye-and-bye."

"Gonna fly in the sweet bye-and-bye."

"Reims?" Franklin said.

He jerked again, like he was startled. "Well...it's the big lawman an' all his pals. How you doin' there, mister big lawman?"

"We're here to see about Miss Marckell. You need to tell us where the body is."

He smiled, and shook his head. "Naw, man. She's mine. She belongs t' me. She my ol' lady." His head sagged, he stared at nothing, and began singing again.

"Gonna die in the sweet bye-and-bye."

"Gonna fly in the sweet bye-and-bye."

43

"Reims!"

Once again he jerked, seemingly confused for a moment. "Huh?"

"She's dead, Reims. You killed her. You'll never leave here alive, so you need to do the right thing and give her up."

"You got it wrong, dude. I'll see her soon. I know the right of it. Gonna sing me free. Gonna walk free after I check out so's I can be with my ol' lady."

"Gonna die in the sweet bye-and-bye."

"Gonna fly in the sweet bye-and-bye."

"If you ever hope to see the light of day, you better loosen up," Harris said.

Reims jerked again, like he'd nodded off. "Huh?"

"It's not too late to get a commutation," Franklin said. "Give her up, we'll talk to the Governor."

"Naw, man, she my ol' lady. You can't have her. I'll be with her once I check out-a here."

"Don't think for one second you'll see her again!" Harris shouted. "The only way you're leaving here is in a casket!"

Reims gave him that twitchy smile. "Yeah, man. Like I said, when I check out-a here. I know the right of it, y'see? Everyone checks out-a here one way or another, then we'll be together, f'ever 'n ever."

"Gonna die in the sweet bye-and-bye."

"Gonna fly in the sweet bye-and-bye."

They leaned on him, hard. Reims just shrugged it off and went on singing. They hounded him about getting his sentence commuted. He ignored them and went on singing. They appealed to his better nature, to give the poor woman peace before he went. Reims just laughed and went on singing. Horton even took him back to one of the solitary confinement cells for some 'old fashioned police work'. That got nowhere, which impressed them since Horton was good at these things. And all the while, Reims kept singing that same aimless, endless ditty:

"Gonna die in the sweet bye-and-bye."

"Gonna fly in the sweet bye-and-bye."

§

"What *is it* with that guy?" Horton griped once they left the prison.

"God, I don't know." Harris stared out the right side window as Franklin drove. "I've seen a lot of hard cases in my time, but that guy..."

"He doesn't care," Franklin said. "He doesn't need to prove anything to anyone, not even himself."

"Then why not give her up?" Harris glanced at Horton, who rubbed his knuckles absently since they were still sore from reasoning with Reims. "No sense in making it any worse on himself."

"They're all like that; bad-asses too tough for the system to handle." Somehow it rang hollow.

There was grim silence as they picked up the state highway and headed south. The headlights of passing cars glistened on the rain-slick pavement, and the gentle hiss of the tires filled their world as they brooded. "Yeah," Harris muttered at last. "How do we get a handle on someone like that?"

"We don't, apparently," Horton said.

"So what do we do?"

"Pray for divine intervention," Clay said.

§

"You're serious?" Archbishop Murdoch's frail build and thin fringe of white hair did nothing to soothe their nervousness. He was well known as an orthodox hard-case. They were all reluctant to even bring this up, Clay more than most, but they'd run out of ideas.

"Yes, Your Eminence, we mean every word of it." Harris was embarrassed and a bit apprehensive, but determined to plow ahead for her sake.

"It does confirm what we've been saying all these years, in a left-handed sort of way," Clay added.

The Archbishop considered them skeptically for a moment. "I guess it does." He leaned back in his chair. "So, you have scientific proof of the existence of a soul which continues after death? We've often been at odds with the scientific community, but this is one case where we can agree."

45

"And Miss Marckell's soul in is danger. She's trapped in some sort of void."

"Her soul is in limbo, Your Eminence, trapped with the body," Clay added.

The Archbishop fixed him with a stern look. "You said the rites for her?"

"Of course, sir. But we didn't have the body to pray over. The evidence suggests we can't free her soul without the body."

Murdoch mused over that. "So what do you want from me?"

"Well...sir..." Clay licked his lips nervously. This was way out in left field, orthodoxically speaking, and the church frowned on revisionism. "We have some blood samples, all the police have recovered thus far. We're hoping you could perform a service for her. With your extra firepower..."

The Archbishop's eyebrow crept up.

"...I know it sounds strange, but we're in unexplored territory here. You may be all she's got."

The Archbishop sighed, and rubbed his eyes. "You know, you people just redefined the soul. I can't help but wonder if this will redefine Heaven, and perhaps God Himself."

§

They gave her the full service with all the bells and whistles. The press were excluded to prevent it from turning into a zoo, but several of her coworkers were there to bear tearful witness to what a good woman she was. The choir performed, a generous collection was raised, and the Archbishop prayed in person over the small casket of bloody rags, begging the Lord with *special* fervor to receive her soul. After that, the casket was buried in the local cemetery, on holy ground, with further prayers and benedictions.

§

They summoned Edwards to bring his machine, and fired it up as soon as he arrived the precinct. "Miss Marckell? This is Lieutenant Franklin. Are you there?"

"Wha...? Who..."

"Miss Marckell, this is Lieutenant Franklin, of the police. Can you hear me?"

46

"Ooohhhh God! Help me! Where am I?" She sounded frantic.

"Miss Marckell! Focus on my voice. We're here to help you."

What emerged was not so much a cry as the wail of a lost soul. The poor woman was coming unglued from sensory deprivation.

"Miss Marckell! Concentrate! Are you still in the dark?"

"I..." She somehow managed to pull herself together enough to answer. "No...nothing's changed. I-I don't feel any different." Her self control was fragile at best. "W-what's happening out there?"

"We thought we had an answer, but it didn't work. We're still trying."

"Please! It's so *empty* here!"

"You have our solemn promise, Miss Marckell! We won't give up on you."

"So what went wrong?" Harris demanded after they signed off.

"I don't know," Doctor Edwards said, defensively. "This is still unexplored territory for us." He brooded on it for a bit, then, "The blood is only a small part of the human body, and you only had samples of that. There may not have been enough."

"So what do we do now?"

Edwards sighed. "Ask him." He gestured at Reverend Clay. "This is more his line."

§

Time dragged on. Doctor Edwards and his machine went back to California. Lieutenant Franklin became a Precinct Captain and left Homicide, and Detective Winston took his place. Sergeant Horton retired. The appeals dragged on up the ladder. A few years later, the 'certain applications' project was canceled, and Edwards' soul-detector gismo became old news. And the fate of Miss Marckell remained on the back burner with all of them. Then the final appeal was turned down by the Supreme Court, and 'Vancouver Johnny' got his date with the needle.

§

Harris dropped by the next day with the bad news. "It looks like Reims will finally get his," he told Franklin.

"Yeah, not that any of us will weep for him," Franklin muttered. "Only..."

Harris nodded glumly. "Only..."

After all this time, Miss Marckell's body was still undiscovered. The rest of the world had chalked it up as a win for the bad guy, but her fate still plagued them. More than that, she'd been in complete sensory deprivation for years; who knew what mental state she was in? Harris was mortally tempted to call Doctor Edwards and have him bring his machine again, but he couldn't bear the thought of what they might discover.

"I don't know what to do any more, Bart."

"We can't just write her off, can we?" That hardly needed answering. Franklin brooded over her fate as he stared absently out the window—streaked with rain—like it was the day so many years ago when they found her purse in that alley. He remembered; the chill he felt then came from no rainy day.

"Well, if we're going to do something we better do it now. The execution is tomorrow, so this is our last crack at him."

§

So they trooped up to the state prison again to work on 'Vancouver Johnny' one more time. Harris was junior DA on that case, so he went along, as did Franklin and Reverend Clay. Joe Horton came out of retirement for this special trip. All of them were haunted by the thought of what Miss Marckell went through, what she was still going through.

'Vancouver Johnny' had been moved to a solitary confinement cell with a solid steel door. Reims was right as they left him, squatting on the floor in lotus position, staring at the wall. What was new was the plastic feeding tube stuck up his nose. His nose was raw and running, but he didn't even notice. He didn't notice his own wastes he sat in, or the vile stench permeating his cell. He just sat there staring at the wall and croaking that damned tune:

"Gonna die in...the sweet bye and bye."

"Gonna fly in the...sweet bye n' bye."

"Gonna die in..."

"Reims?"

"...the sweet bye and bye..."

"Reims!"

"...Gonna fly in the..."

"Reims! Wake up!"

The singing tapered off, and Reims stared aimlessly at the wall as he slowly came back.   Finally, he blinked several times and shook his head spasmodically, as if wakened out of a deep sleep.

"Reims!"

"Huh?" Reims stared at them stupidly.

Harris turned to the duty sergeant. "What's with this guy? He's stoned! How'd he get a fix?"

The sergeant was properly pissed at that accusation. "He ain't stoned. He's like that all the time, day and night, singin' that same damned tune. God, it's driving us all crazy. That's why we stuck him in here, so we don't have to hear him." He fixed Harris with a cold glare. "And he ain't gettin' no drugs in here. What's he got to trade for 'em, anyway, huh?"

He was right, Harris realized.

"What you want, man?" Reims whined.

"You have one last chance to do the right thing, Reims," Harris said, evenly. "You're going to get the needle. You need to tell us where her body is. She needs to be laid to rest."

"Man, you make me tired...tol' you, she my woman."   He drifted off and started mumbling his tune again.

"Gon die ina...swee bye n bye..."

"Gonna..."

"REIMS!"   Harris grabbed his shoulder and shook him.   He flopped around like a rag doll. "Wake up!"

"Huh? Hay...wha...?" It took him even longer to come back than before. "*What*, man?"

"You don't get how serious this is, *man!* You're going to get the needle. You can still save yourself if you play ball."

"No shit, *man*. Why I wanna do that, huh? I'm all set t' check out-a here."   Reims gave them that twitchy smile.   "Gonna drink the Gov'nor's cocktail," he muttered. That jittery smile crept across his face, and his eyes lit up. "Cocktails wit' the Gov'nor. Be some good shit, man.   Best fix a guy can get."   He settled in lotus position and began singing again, completely ignoring them.

"Gonna...die ina swee...bye n bye..."

"Gon fly ina...sweet bye n bye..."

§

Desperation time.   DA Harris drove all night to the state capital, and confronted the Governor the first thing the next morning with the wildest story he'd heard in his thirty years in politics.

"You want me to commute his sentence to *life?*"

Harris took a deep breath and said, "I want you to pardon him. He might give up the body if we let him go."

The Governor looked askance at him. "Are you crazy, Doug?"

"This whole damned thing is crazy!"   Harris fought to get himself under control. "We have a whole new wrinkle to the law here. This is something we've never had to face before. We have to cut him a deal to get her body back so we can give her the Last Rites."

"This is ridiculous. You don't really *believe* this nonsense, do you?"

"We have to help her! She's stuck in her body! She's going crazy!"

"Looks to me like you're going crazy, Doug."

Harris sighed and rubbed his eyes trying to relieve his fatigue headache. "Yeah, I probably am. This whole thing has us all so messed up. Look...we cut him loose on the murder, he gives us the body, then we extradite him back to Washington so they can have a crack at him. They have a murder case there, too. With this new psychic technology, they can get a conviction."

"On the sworn testimony of the victim in a murder case?"

"What about Miss Marckell?" Horton asked, tensely. "He's her only hope."

The Governor shook his head.   "Sorry, Dave.   There's no scientific basis for your claim, and the law is the law. More than that, it'd be political suicide for both of us. If I turn him loose, the reporters will have our heads, even if he doesn't go off on someone else."

"This is not about some damned election!"

"It's *always* about some damned election!" the Governor roared. "You know the public will never understand. All they'll see is us caving in to a psychopath."

§

Having struck out with the Governor, Harris tried his luck with the Chief Justice of the State Court.

"And here I thought I'd seen it all," he said, bemused.

"Please...I need a stay of execution. *She* needs a stay so we can work on him."

The Chief Justice shook his head. "I'm sorry, Dave. It's out of my jurisdiction since the ruling came down from the Supremes."

"Then grant me a temporary stay to offer new evidence."

"What new evidence? The fact that you can talk with the dead? Can she give you an exculpatory statement?"

"...No. If anything, her testimony would finish him."

"Even if she could clear the guy, her testimony isn't admissible. The law doesn't cover something like this. You've opened a huge can of worms, you realize?"

"Take a number," Harris sighed. "Isn't there *anything* you can do for her?"

"Well..." the Chief Justice mused over it in disbelief. "I'll pass it over to Federal with my recommendation, but I'll tell you right now, they won't buy this; not after all they went through to put him down."

§

Harris arrived at the State Prison about an hour before the execution, bleary-eyed from lack of sleep, strung out on C-store coffee, and frazzled by his endless fretting. Franklin, Horton, Clay, and Doctor Albert were already there, joined by the prison chaplain, Reverend Howard.

"So what do we do?" Franklin asked when Harris gave them the bad news.

Harris sighed, and rubbed his eyes in exasperation. "No idea. We keep looking for her body, of course..."

"And what are the odds on that?"

Harris considered him for a moment, then shook his head. They'd dug up half the county already, with nothing to show for it.

"He...knows where she's buried..." Clay said.

"And he won't talk," Horton snapped, irritably. "We can't intimidate him, we can't bribe him, we can't beat it out of him."

"Could we drug him, maybe? Sodium Pentothal..."

51

Harris had to focus to answer that one. "To start with, it's not legal. And with all the heat on this case, you'd never keep it secret. And second, with all the drugs he's done, would it make a difference?"

Doctor Albert fielded that one. "I doubt it. I was up there a while ago. He stares at nothing and sings that damned tune over and over. He hardly responds to external stimulus any more. He doesn't eat, he doesn't drink, he doesn't sleep. He doesn't even notice the feeding tube up his nose. He just sits there and sings 24/7. He's so whacked out that sodium probably wouldn't faze him."

"More withdrawn than ever," Harris muttered. "He's spacing out on that song as the execution gets closer."

"Damn! He'll miss the show," Franklin grumbled. "If there was ever a scumbag who deserved to sweat the last few minutes, he's the one."

"Yeah, well at least he'll stop singing in another twenty minutes," Horton grumbled. "Sick bastard. Serves him right."

"It's a shame about Miss Marckell," Albert said. "We won't give up on her. We'll find her eventually." They all knew they were whistling past the proverbial graveyard.

Then Reverend Clay turned pale. Horton noticed. "What?"

"He...said he would join her after he checks out of here, that they'd be together forever," he muttered. His eyes were sick and hollow. "He knows where she is. He knows where to find her after he's dead."

That amped the tension in the room: Reims would be free to do whatever he wanted to her, and the law was helpless to stop him. "Well, then, we just don't give him Last Rites." Horton gave the Chaplain a hard look. "Let him sweat in solitary for a while, then offer him a deal for her body."

"Gonna fly in the sweet bye-and-bye," Doctor Albert muttered. "He beat you to the punch, Joe."

"Huh?"

"That hymn he keeps singing; he's performing his own Last Rites."

Horton was confused. "I don't get it."

52

"Many cultures have out-of-body rituals involving mind-altering drugs and self hypnosis."   Albert had done extensive research on the matter.   "He said he knew the right of it.   All those street drugs must have shown him the secret.   Acid, Angel Dust, Peyote..."

"He's...gonna set himself free?"   There was a grim silence as they absorbed this new setback.   "Dammit, you mean he'll beat the rap on this?"

"'Fraid so.   Look how spaced he is already.   His psyche is clinging to his body by its fingernails."

"So what do we do?"

Harris sighed, and shook his head.   He was tempted to call Doctor Edwards to bring his machine so they could at least warn her—but—he glanced at the clock: it was too late for that.   "We keep looking for the body, and pray."

§

At one minute past midnight, after ten long years of litigation, John 'Vancouver Johnny' Reims got his last fix.   Within seconds, far sooner than expected, he was dead.

*****

So: man has dominion over the earth and all things of the earth, and truly is Lord Of All He Surveys—or so the riff goes. A comforting theory, that. It makes one feel all warm and fuzzy inside, as if we were ordained somehow. But what if the theory is wrong...?

"Superpredator"

Reflections On Life And Death: Pondering Man's Place In Nature. *Lymon Fuller. Cambridge: Harvard UP, 2028.*

For at least the last two-and-a-half million years, ever since we first figured out how to use a rock as a weapon, humans have had a unique relationship with the ecosystem. And this has not been a happy relationship, for we have become superpredators: creatures so deadly no other life form can stand against us. If Tyrannosaurus Rex were still around, he would be on the Endangered Species List, along with the tiger, the codfish, and the plague bacillus. If that statement sounds remarkable, the story of how we achieved this power is equally remarkable.

Viewed as natural beings, we are weak. Our early hominid ancestors were weaker. We are not particularly strong or fast or agile, our senses are mediocre, and our birth rate is dangerously low. Were it not for our toolmaking intellect, we would probably be extinct, as are most of the ancestral hominids who once competed with us. But that unique intellect—that quirk of fate or random mutation—makes all the difference. What we lack in muscles, teeth, and claws, we make up in organization, strategy, and technology. Millions of years ago we figured out how to pick up a rock, and make fire, and chip flint; and with these high-tech marvels, we slaughtered our way to the top of the food chain.

We take a certain foolish pride in this accomplishment, although if you think about it, it is actually cause for alarm. For, you see, we are no longer a part of nature. We are no longer subject to nature's checks and balances. Instead, we consume nature; absorbing all in our path; converting land, minerals, energy, whole species into our own little ecosystem for one. Indeed, it is now clear that if we keep going as we are, we will eventually destroy nature, rendering the earth a sterile desert. Truly, the superpredator—the tool making intellect—is the cancer of ecosystems.

Normally, we think of cancer as a fatal condition, and if you have any sense of shame, you might weep a tear for the Monarch Butterfly and the Manatee. But life will endure. Life will adapt. Species come and species go. Old T. Rex was spared our tender mercies by a cataclysmic great extinction, lucky stiff, and his place in the ecosystem was taken by the enormous terror birds, and they in turn by the sabertooths. That's the way it works: species come and species go, but nature itself—life as we know it—goes on.

Life is the ultimate force, capable of surviving anything which doesn't shatter the earth entirely. Life is found in the frozen arctic, in volcanos, in the crushing depths of the sea. Life thrives where we 'advanced' hominids would perish instantly. Indeed, life as we know it evolved on a world utterly unfit for life—and remade it to serve. Life is tenacious, the ultimate survivor, and life will do whatever it must to survive, even if it means excising the cancer.

That is the true horror of the moment millions of years ago when our Australopithecine ancestor first became a tool user. For nothing can stand against a superpredator: no creature, no disease, no matter how deadly, could hope to restore us to our proper place in the balance of nature. Having been cast out of Paradise, we can never go back again.

So the pressure will build until something gives. There will come a day when the pressure of nature becomes so great that it can no longer be contained by mere artifice. There will come a day when our tool-making intellect will face the final confrontation with the forces which turned this barren rock into a Garden Of Eden, and despite our presumptions, we are not the stronger.

We have had a long and frighteningly successful reign on this world, but species come and species go, and nature will do what it must to survive. And the only thing which could save this world from us would be another—deadlier—superpredator.

*****

55

Wish fulfillment: the favorite subject of daydreams, romantic longing, and fantasy fiction. None of us are truly happy with our lot, and wish we could change things for the better. But there are good reasons why wishes rarely come true, and why we press that particular envelope at our peril...

"Wishful Thinking"

Ireland was turning out to be a *big* disappointment, and after four days in this sodden, rain-soaked miscarriage, Wilbur was about fed up. The locals were friendly enough, if one was careful to avoid certain topics, but the 'quaint' country village where the tour group went to ground in a local bed-and-breakfast offered precious little entertainment value other than schmoozing at the local pub.

"I paid three thousand for this?" he muttered as he surveyed the soggy countryside around him.

Those lovely travel posters conveniently failed to mention *why* Ireland is so green: it rained constantly here. Not only was the grass green, and the trees, but every other color was smothered in a clinging coat of moss. Rocks, trees, fences, it was all green. Wilbur used to like green, but lately he was getting a bit tired of it.

"...ahhh...aaaahhhh...aaahhhh...*CHOOO!* Dammit!"

And on top of *everything* else, he had the mother of all head colds, not surprising in this damp chill. His sinuses were in agony and he had a pounding headache, but what really worried him was his chronic cough. "Damn fool! You'll probably get pneumonia," he grumbled to himself. "You should know better."

It was like this every year, every damned year. He spent all year working his freakin' *ass* off trying to save up a little money, only to go and blow it on one of these overseas guided tours. *Anything* to get out of New York City! His neighbor, an inveterate Son of the Old Sod, suggested a tour of Ireland, and fool that he was, he took him up on it. It *was* a change from the Big Apple anyway, and at least he was in no danger of getting heat stroke like he did in Egypt last time.

"...ahhh...aaaahhhh...aaahhhh...*CHOOO!* Shit!"

He tugged his jacket tighter against the chill and dug his hands into his pockets, silently cursing his penchant for poor vacation choices. There was no—none, nada, zip—action here. The local girls on the whole were rather *substantial*, and not inclined to indulge his advances. At least he wasn't risking another case of VD like he got in Singapore, not that he appreciated his good fortune. The beer was boring, the food greasy, and his room at the BnB drafty. Even his present walk in the countryside, an act of desperation, was unsatisfactory. The rest of the tour were off visiting the local monastery—*booorrring*—so he was left to wander the backest of back roads in search of some distraction.

"...ahhh...aaaahhhh...aaahhhh...*CHOOO!* Sumbitch!"

He dug the paper napkin out of his pocket once again, but it was already a sodden mess. He tossed it aside in disgust and tried to decide which sleeve was the less soaked.

"...ahhh...aaaahhhh...aaahhhh...*CHOOO!*"   He sighed in frustration as he wiped his upper lip. "It's my own damn fault, I guess."

It was a moment before he heard a faint sound, like the cry of an injured animal from somewhere nearby. It didn't register at first, but when it came again, he started wondering. If he didn't know better, it sounded like a faint voice. It *was* a voice! Someone was hurt and calling for help.

The countryside thereabouts was rolling, and the trail wound along the base of a low cliff. Up ahead, just around a bend, a section of the cliff had crumbled, dumping a small avalanche onto the road. That avalanche claimed a victim: a short, rotund little man dressed in a green jacket and knee breeches lay pinned under a flat slab of rock.

If he could have stood, he would be about a foot tall.

"What the...*hell* are you?" Wilbur asked in amazement.

The little man gave him a venomous look. "Wha' d'ye think I am? I'm a leprechaun, ye barmy fool! Get this blooody great rock off me. Ah swear me ribs is cracked!"

"Oh. Sure." That rock was a daunting prospect, but he planted his feet carefully and strained. The rock shifted a bit.

"That's it, man. A wee bit more." The leprechaun was struggling to extract himself from under the boulder.

Wilbur strained even more, and the rock shifted fractionally. "I'll probably rupture myself," he grumbled. "Just my luck." He held on grimly as the leprechaun dragged himself between his legs to safety, and finally lay flat on the ground gasping for breath.

It was only then Wilbur began to appreciate how *weird* this scene was. He just rescued a freakin' *leprechaun!* He'd heard stories about the Wee Folk since he was a kid, and always dismissed them as superstitious twaddle, only here was the real deal laying in the road right before his eyes. Said leprechaun gasped for air, with a streak of blood—bright red, fancy that—on his chin. Obviously he was hurt and in pain. After a moment, he muttered something Wilbur couldn't catch, then relaxed with a heart-felt sigh.

"Are you all right?"

The leprechaun finally turned his attention to his rescuer. "Ach, me boyo, tis me undying gratitude ye have, for sure!"

"You're hurt! Do you need a doctor?"

The leprechaun pressed his ribs gently with one hand. "I'll be right as rain presently. The spells act fast enough." He struggled to his feet, gathered up his tiny hat and walking stick, and straightened his green jacket, then took a couple deep breaths. "Aye, that's nae so bad a'tall. The pain's all but gone." He eyed the rockslide uneasily, then turned to Wilbur again. "Well, it's been a pleasure laddie, but ah need t' be off so if ye'll excuse me..."

"Wait a minute! Aren't I supposed to get some wishes for helping you?"

The leprechaun hesitated. "Aye," he said at last, somberly. "Ye've caught me out. Since ye've done me a good turn, ye can have Three Wishes back to ye in repayment."

"Three wishes, huh?" *This* was more like it! All of a sudden Wilbur's miscarried Irish vacation had become interesting. "I can have anything I wish for?"

"Aye, that ye can." Said leprechaun didn't seem thrilled at being 'caught out'.

"Alright! I wish for a billion dollars."

"Ummmmm...no."

"*No?*"

"Ye canna have that."

"But that's what I wished for! You said I could have anything I wanted."

"Well, perhaps I was a bit hasty. Ye can have Three Wishes *provided* they're things we're willin' t' grant."

"So why can't I have a billion?"

"Because that sort o' thing attracts attention. How're ye goin' t' explain your sudden wealth t' yer gov'ment, eh? Ye'll tell 'em a leprechaun gifted it t' ye?"

"Uh...good point." They'd probably figure he was a drug kingpin. Don't need the narcs kicking *his* door down.

"And that sort o' thing draws attention t' the Wee Folk," the leprechaun added. "We dinna want our countryside swarmin' wi' treasure hunters wavin' butterfly nets."

"Oh." Wilbur was momentarily stumped. "Well...how about I have the undying love of the most beautiful woman in the world?"

The leprechaun sighed and nodded morosely. "Aye, tis one of the most sought-after wishes of them all, but not real practical, ye know?"

"Why not?"

"First, because there are a host o' 'most beautiful' women; it depends on yer ideal of beauty. D'ye really want the undying passion of *thousands* of women?"

"Um..." That didn't sound bad at all, in fact.

"Second, most of these 'most beautiful' women have husbands, and most of *them* are powerful men—dictators an' rich capitalists an' the like. Women that grand tend t' marry up, ye know. D'ye want those men t' come lookin' for ye fer stealin' their women?"

Right. Of course. Queens would be logjammed with all the hit-men and corporate goons after his scalp. There's always a catch.

"Well, okay, forget it. Can you make me famous? Can you make me into a Hollywood A-list actor?"

The leprechaun eyed him skeptically. "Can ye act?"

"Um..."

"Ah thought not. Ye canna have that either, boyo."

"Well *why not?*"

"Because I'm nae about t' spend the rest of yer life spoon feeding every word t' come out-a yer mouth! If ye haven't got it, ah canna fake it for ye."

"Why am I not surprised?"

"In any event, ah'm nae so great an actor meself, so ye'll need t' try again."

Wilbur was momentarily stumped. "Um... How about can you bring my grandmother back to life?"

"Aye, we can do that," the leprechaun said, gravely. "But d'ye really want t' do that t' her?"

"What do you mean?"

"How long ago did she die?"

"About twenty years."

"She'd be over a hundred now. And her health...what did she die of?"

"She had a bad heart."

"And she'll still have it, along with arthritis and brittle bones and she'll likely be senile, too. Would ye do that t' yer sainted grandmum?"

Wilbur recoiled at the thought. "No, that wouldn't do at all. So what *can* I wish for?"

"Anythin' ye want, laddie. Wi' certain *provisions*."

"Provisions, huh? I suppose that means I can't wish for three more wishes?"

"Aye, nor for three more leprechauns, either. We figured that one long ago."

"Um...how about me becoming President of the United States?"

The leprechaun gave him a sour look. "Ye dinna have much self respect, do ye?"

"*What?*"

"D'ye really want t' wallow in that slime? Wi' all the hate an' vilification poured on ye? Wi all the corruption, an' all those parasites hangin' on t' yer coat tails seekin' special favors?"

"Um...

"D'ye really want the twenty hour days? And the endless crises? D'ye want every lunatic in the land gunnin' for ye?"

"Alright all ready! Jeez!"

"It'd be over in four years anyway, unless ye were truly unlucky. An' what would ye do wi' yerself then?"

"...ahhh...aaaahhhh...aaahhhh...*CHOOO!* Can you at least stop this damned rain?" It was pouring at the moment, and Wilbur was soaked to the bone.

"No, laddie, that's one thing we'll nae do for anything."

"Why the hell not? This weather is miserable!"

"For the likes of ye maybe, but the Wee Folk love this weather." That wasn't fair: the little man was perfectly dry and comfortable despite the downpour.

By now Wilbur was ready to tear his hair out in frustration. "Tell me something," he demanded. "Why do you leprechauns have all the fun? Why can't we humans grant wishes too?"

The leprechaun paused to size him up somberly. "That would'na be wise, as ye've seen. The Saints granted us the Power for our own uses since we ha' the wit nae t' go chargin' about like so many drunken Fenians. We developed the tradition of helpin' the Big Folk on occasion, but it's only from the goodness o' our hearts an' our sense o' fair play."

"How do the locals do this? Surely *some* of them have been granted wishes at *some* time. What do they wish for?"

"Mostly they don't. They know better."

Wilbur nodded in resignation. "That figures."

"Come along now, laddie," the leprechaun said, impatiently. "I ha'na all day. Make yer wishes if ye're goin' to or I'll be off and ye'll forfeit the lot."

"But what can I do? Nothing I wish for works."

The leprechaun pondered him for a bit. "Well laddie, if ye'll listen t' the voice of experience, it'd say t' think small. Wish for practical things, and leave yer wild imaginings for yer daydreams."

"Ah, yeah. I guess." Wilbur thought it over and came to a decision. "Well for starters, this trip has been a real disappointment—not that Ireland isn't a lovely place! It's just not my style. I'd like my three thousand dollars back."

"Aye, now yer bein' sensible!" The leprechaun pointed his walking stick at Wilbur and wiggled his nose. "Done!"

Wilbur felt a sudden lump in his jacket picket. He dug in, and came up with a roll of crisp new hundred dollar bills. "Well I'll be damned!"

"Dinna tempt fate, laddie."

"Um...yeah. Thanks for the payday." He pocketed the wad again.

"So what about yer Second Wish?"

"Um...okay. I'd like...ahhh...aaaahhhh...aaahhhh...*CHOOO!* Damn this cold!" He wiped his runny nose on his sleeve. "Enough of this! For my second wish, I want to never have a cold again, ever."

"That seems reasonable." The leprechaun pointed his walking stick and wiggled his nose again. "Done!"

And just like that, the pressure in his sinuses was gone. He took a deep, invigorating breath and let it out with a sigh. His nose was clear, the ache in his throat gone, his headache vanquished. "Great! You should bottle that. You'd make a fortune! Thanks."

"Tis nothin', laddie. Now what about yer Third Wish?"

"Um..." Wilbur hesitated, thinking furiously. This was his last shot, and all he had to show for it thus far was a lousy three grand and an unstuffed nose. He needed to score big...but that *friggin'* leprechaun kept cutting him off at the knees. Can't go *too* big... What to wish for? A parade of his deepest longings and frustrations passed before his mind's eye, taunting him. So near, yet so far. What to wish for? It was some minutes before he finally decided he was stuck.

"Jeez...there's so *many* things I want, I can't decide."

"Tis a quandary fer sure."

"I tell you, it really grates on my nerves at times to think of how *little* I have in life. I work my fingers to the *bone*, and what do I have to show for it? Sometimes I wonder why I bother."

"Ah can see that. It seems t' me ye thinks too much. You city types are all alike: fussin' and' frettin' an' schemin' the whole day through. Tis nae wonder ye're so down at the mouth. Ye need t' simplify yer life before it drives ye barmy."

"God, you got that right!" Wilbur finally realized what he needed more than anything. "I've been miserable all along chasing those damned rainbows."

"Money, fame, power—they're snares an' delusions, lad. They ne'er satisfy the inner need. Ye need t' let go an' seek peace wi'in yerself."

"All I really want is to be happy." Revelation dawned on him, filling him with new hope. He turned to the leprechaun imploringly. "Please, can you make me happy?"

"Ah... That's...nae so simple..."

"But you could do it? You could make me happy?"

"Aye..."

"Well then, that's my third wish."

"But..."

"No buts! If I can't find a little happiness in this life, then what's the use of living? You can at least give me that!"

"It's more somethin' t' seek wi'in yerself..."

"Why waste the effort when you could do it for me? *You* can make me happy. I did you a favor after all; you owe me this!"

The leprechaun sighed. "Alright, laddie. Tis against me better judgment, but if that's wha ye truly want, then so be it."

"That's what I truly want. I want to be completely happy for the rest of my life."

"Foolish mortal. If that's yer Third Wish, then ye'll have it, but don't blame me of it's nae t' yer liking!" The leprechaun pointed his walking stick and wiggled his nose once more. "Done!"

§

Wilbur's sister came to visit him in the hospital six months later, which was never an easy thing for her. He seemed to recognize her as usual, nodding and smiling vaguely when she spoke to him, but he never answered. He was like that all the time: he smiled at pleasant things like sunsets or music or flowers, but otherwise sat staring at nothing, oblivious to the world around him.

"Has there been any change?" she asked his doctor later.

His doctor greeted that with a sour expression. "I'm afraid there's been no improvement. He continues to exhibit a severely reduced intellect; we still have no idea why." He wasn't going to tell her what one of his exasperated co-workers said earlier: *'He has the IQ of a house plant!'*. You don't *say* things like that to grieving relatives, even if it's true enough.

"I *wish* there was something you could do!"

"It's a mystery. There's no evidence of head trauma, no viral infection, no trace of disease, no strokes, no toxins...nothing. His reflexes, bodily functions, and EEG readings are entirely normal, only there's very little higher brain activity. Honestly, we're at a loss."

Wilbur had become a medical phenomenon, in fact. There was a lively and nervous debate in medical-psychological circles over what caused his condition, and he was the subject of several high priority research projects. They had given up on finding a cure by then, and were worried about preventing it from happening to anyone else. Not that Wilbur knew or cared. He sat in his chair by the window each day nodding and smiling at the birds on the lawn and the clouds drifting past. He especially enjoyed the rain.

"The only thing I can think of is he must have gotten ahold of some bad home brew." The doctor was grasping at straws, but then they all were. "He was found wandering the countryside in rural Ireland in his present state. I *wish* we could know what happened to him there."

She nodded dolefully. "Yes. He wandered off from his tour group. Is there any hope for him?"

The doctor shook his head reluctantly. "I don't see how, unless there's a miracle..."

She paused to watch Wilbur sitting by the window nodding and smiling vaguely. "Well, at least he seems happy. That's some consolation."

*****

Divine Justice: we've all heard of it. Some discount the concept, some fear it, some long for it, and some deserve it —or not. The thing to keep in mind, of course, is that Things Which Go 'Bump' In The Night don't necessarily have to be big to be scary...

"Innocent"

I was pretty well wasted by time I got home. Work was hell that day, with no end of hassles and headaches, and the Super riding my sorry ass like it was the Kentucky Derby. It was well after dark when I trudged up the steps to my apartment building, keyed myself in, and stopped at my mail box. Nothing but junk and the evening paper, which I carried along without bothering to look at it.

The hallway smelled of dust and greasy cooking, like always, and a radio in one of the apartments was playing an old cool jazz number:

> *'Momma said there'd be days like this.'*
> *'There'd be days like this, momma said.'*

"Gawd, you know it," I muttered as I sidestepped some kid's tricycle. Right then all I wanted was to get something to eat, and get to bed.

I fumbled the door key and flicked the light switch...

...nothing.

"Shit." The bulb was burned out. The room was dimly lit by the street lamps, so I threw the mail on the bed, inched my way along the wall to the kitchen and groped for the switch...

...nothing.

"They won't work," a soft voice came out of the gloom. "None of them will work for you any more, ever."

And just like that I wasn't tired. This wasn't the best neighborhood; I instinctively grabbed a kitchen knife out of the wooden block in a flash of near panic.

"Who's there?"

65

"You think that impresses me?" The voice was soft, a girl or young woman, but it was utterly flat, devoid of life. "You think you can scare me with your big, bad knife now?"

"Who are you? What do you want?"

"You may not remember me from all the others, but you should know what I want." A shadow stirred across the main room, and a dim figure emerged from the gloom. "This isn't over."

That was a relief in a way; she was a mere slip of a girl, not more than five foot three, and slender. I kept her covered with the kitchen knife while I looked her over quickly. There was no sign of a gun. "Who are you? What are you doing here?"

"You never bother to know, do you?" Her voice was flat, without emotion. Scary. "It didn't matter who I was, did it? But you should know why I'm here, at least."

I figured she must be on drugs or something, the way she carried on. At least she seemed harmless. She hovered in the shadows in the far corner of the room, and I realized I must have interrupted a burglary, and she was waiting her chance to break for the door. That was fine by me. "Enough of this! You get out of here or I'll call a cop!"

"Go ahead. Call them. They're looking for you. Not that giving yourself up will help you now. This is just between you and me."

That wasn't what I expected, and it should have alerted me that something was *wrong*, but I was coming down off my panic reaction and starting to get mad. "You and me, huh? Lady, we got nothing between you and me. I never saw you before, and I don't want to see you now."

"You liked what you saw before, after you were through with me. You gloated over me. Why wouldn't you like to see me now?"

She stepped further out of the shadows into the faint light coming through the window. That was when I saw her face and neck were a battered pulp. Her lips were swollen, one eye almost shut, huge bruises on her neck, and her shirt and slacks were drenched in blood. *"What th' hell happened to you?"*

"You did. This is why I'm here. But you know that already."

"What? *Are you crazy?*"

"Probably, after what you did to me."

"What I did? I did no such thing! I never even met you."

"It won't do you any good. I know the truth."

"You know nothing! You just get out of here!" I was unnerved enough to act; taking two quick strides across the room, intending to give her the bum's rush, and grabbed her shoulder...

...and my hand went right through her like she wasn't there. I jerked back in panic, and my arm went through her shoulder again. I didn't feel a thing, and she stood unmoving through it all. "What th' hell?" I poked at her gingerly, but my fingers swam right through her chest. "What is this?"

"This is justice." She looked up at me with her battered features twisted in rage. "You can't hurt me any more. Now it's my turn; for me and the others."

"Wha? Who are you?! *What are you?!*"

"You really don't remember? Not surprising, what with the rage you were in." She gestured at the paper laying on the bed. "See for yourself."

That confused me, dampening my anger. I stared at her for a moment, wondering what the hell was going on, then glanced at the rolled up newspaper. See for myself? Without willing it, I picked it up and pulled the rubber band off. The headline slapped me in the face:

Serial Killer Strikes Again
Fifth Victim Found.

Leslie Ann Harper, 20 years old, is the latest victim of the Midtown Mauler after her body was discovered this morning in an alley off 43rd street. An FBI investigator is quoted as saying, "This is one of the most horrific crime scenes I've witnessed in a long time."

"You hurt me," she said, emotionlessly. "What you did hurt so bad, but it's nothing compared to what you're going to feel."

"What?" I stared aghast at the screaming headline, then at her battered features. "What does this have to do with me?"

"Don't deny it. You know what you did. At least be honest with yourself."

Then I realized what was going on, and I was scared even more. "Look...ah...Leslie, you got the wrong guy..."

"Don't you EVER say my name!" It was her first display of emotion, and it lit her up like a fiend. "You don't *deserve* to say my name! Ever!"

"B-but you got it wrong! I'm not the one you're after! Leslie...AAAaaaaahhhhhh!" My protest was cut short by a searing pain which split me from crotch to navel.

"That was when you slit me open, after you raped me." She stood over me as I lay helpless on the floor curled around my agony. "Every time you say my name, I'll do that to you again."

"B-but...I'm...not..."

"Don't you think the memory of you would be imprinted on me forever?" I reeled under a series of savage blows to the face coming from nowhere. "Don't you think I'd know you even in a dark alley? We have a score to settle, for what you did to me and the others." I was choking, gagging as my windpipe was crushed by unseen hands. "How do you like it? Can't take what you can dish out, can you?"

I don't know how long it went on, but finally it was over. She stepped back by the window as I lay on the floor, numb and trembling, trying to get a handle on it. She was a ghost! I wouldn't have believed it, but there she was: a *freakin'* ghost. My dazed mind was spinning, trying to figure out why she would pick on me. Could I *possibly* have done it? I didn't remember any of it. Was I some kind of sleep-walking psychopath? It didn't seem possible. I never found any bloody clothing in the mornings, and I did well enough with the ladies that I didn't need to go hunting them in dark alleys. The real horror of what was going on sank in then: she was driven mad by what happened to her, out for blood vengeance, and she'd latched onto me by mistake! The pain was unbelievable, but when I groped my abdomen, there was no blood. Then the horror of what was happening to *me* hit home: I wouldn't die from this unless I had a heart attack. And I just knew, without asking, I wouldn't be so lucky.

"I suppose they'll take you to a nut-house eventually." Her voice was cool, with a hint of vindictive rage. "They can't see me, and they won't believe you if you tell them about me. They'll figure you finally went off the deep end after killing us, and they'll lock you up." I gagged as a searing pain went through my chest. "That was when you cut my teats off."

"...please..." I gasped for air as my pulse pounded. I realized vaguely that I'd messed myself.

"Begging won't save you. You're about to get the justice you deserve. I'll be here, every night, in the shadows. I'll be here for the rest of your miserable life, and I'll be here afterwards." She leaned down and looked in my face with expressionless, dead eyes. "Now it's your turn to fear the dark!"

I gasped for breath. "But...why?"

She shrugged. "I don't understand it either." Her voice was flat and emotionless again. "Maybe it's Divine Justice, or maybe this is your personal hell. Either way, you've run up a bill, and I've been chosen to collect."

She withdrew for a bit and stood staring out the window, outlined by the faint light, tears rolling down her cheeks. She must have been a pretty little thing once; sweet and innocent; a magnet for a sexual predator. She shifted slightly, and the street light shown through her. She was trapped in her worst nightmare, just like me. The light would never be the same for her again. I felt sorry for her, but I had my own pain and fear to deal with.

"You know the sad thing about this?" She turned to face me. "I used to be a nice person, really sweet. All I ever wanted was to work in the book store and meet some decent guy and raise a family." Her voice took on an edge again. "But then you came along. You changed me. You took away my future. You took away the children I'll never have. You took away my soul, made me into what I am."

I managed to struggle up on one shoulder and looked at this slip of a girl...this mad ghost sworn to eternal vengeance...and wondered how long I'd last. With my luck, it'd be a good long time. A faint sound intruded then; a radio in one of the apartments playing an old cool jazz number:

'Momma said there'd be days like this.'
'There'd be days like this, momma said.'

She cocked her ear to the tune, and nodded to herself. "Do you believe in God?"

"Huh?"

"I used to, kind of. I never was sure. Now I am. *He* found me, after you were through, and made me the instrument of His justice. Why me? Didn't I suffer enough?" she sobbed bitterly. "I...guess I was drafted for this job." Her voice turned hard again. "You took away that sweet person. You gave me what I'll need to make you pay for your crimes, forever. But I'll never be able to rest, either. Forever! That's something else I will *never* forgive you for!"

I used to believe as well, sort of, but I realized that I could never believe again: God would never allow a screw-up like this to go down. I was on my own with this mad bitch. Forever. Unless I could somehow talk her down. It seemed hopeless, but the alternative was to spend eternity being carved up by her memories. That's a powerful incentive. I managed to struggle to a sitting position on the floor in front of her. "Look...I'm not the one you want...I'm sorry for what happened to you..."

Invisible hands around my throat stopped me. As I lay there gagging, she leaned down and studied my face with her dead eyes. "No, you're not. Not yet. But you will be."

She was right about that, at least.

*****

There will always be those who wish to topple the established order for reasons good or evil. Governments guard their positions jealously, and never hesitate to act swiftly against potential usurpers. The problem, of course, is that the means of revolution are not always obvious...

"A Matter Of Taste"

August, 1910:

"We are most gratified by your interest in our company, Doctor Marquaid." Andrew Beauford was uncertain whether to offer his hand, not because he feared this mysterious clergyman would refuse it, but that his companion might not. "If World Wide Flavors can help you, we are pleased to do so."

"Thank you, sir." This Reverend Marquaid had an odd accent, English to be certain, but with an exotic flavor as if that was not his first language. "Our backers have been following your progress and we feel you may be able to provide us with the solution we have been seeking."

He was tall and slender as a rail, with wiry muscles, a weather-beaten complexion and eyes which constantly roamed the area, giving him the look of a jungle predator. One might easily mistake him for an explorer just returned from the wild in an ill-fitting Panama suit...were it not for the clerical collar. His companion was, to say the least, even more exotic: clearly a native from the jungles of South America. That one was short, dark, and muscular, and if Doctor Marquaid had a wild look in his eyes, his cohort, though dressed in an identical Panama suit, was the personification of a feral man. He stood silently at his patron's side, unmoving, unsmiling, unspeaking, but his eyes missed nothing, and there was an explosive tension in him which was palpable.

But to business; Andrew shook off the distraction and put on an only *somewhat* forced smile. "And, ah, how may World Wide Flavors be of service to you?"

"We are interested in these artificial foods you are perfecting." Doctor Marquaid spread his arm in an expansive gesture taking in the display shelves in Andrew's small office. "I represent the

World Humanity League, an organization dedicated to helping the native peoples of the world adapt to living with modern society. One of the biggest problems we have is in the diets of those native peoples. We feel your artificial foods may be the solution to that long-standing problem."

"I...fear I do not understand the problem, sir." Andrew couldn't help a nervous glance at Marquaid's native companion. "The tropics must have have an abundance of foods, and the...ah...local people surely have no problem in finding them."

Indeed, until that moment, he had not given a thought to anything beyond their immediate situation. World Wide Flavors was tiny and deeply in debt, and their artificial flavors were only now gaining acceptance in the marketplace. In fact, were it not for the Great War in Europe and the droughts and repeated crop failures brought on by the explosion of so many atom weapons back in 1905, World Wide Flavors would never have gotten off the ground. The company had more than its share of problems attracting capital and fighting off the potent farm and cattle lobbies, and he had given little thought to possible world markets.

"I can assure you, sir, the real problem is political," Marquaid said. "Most native peoples of the world are controlled by the great European empires, which have long sought to suppress the native cultures. Aiding these people is more complex than simply offloading so many bags of rice!" A bitter edge crept into his voice, and even his native companion seemed ill at ease. "It is our hope that your new artificial foods will provide an acceptable alternative to the natives' traditional diets, which will reduce their unrest and allow them to relate to Europeans more easily."

"Your proposal sounds most convoluted." Andrew said, doubtfully, "But I am certain you have given this far more thought than your few words suggest."

"We know our course of action clearly, sir."

"Indeed. Then allow me to show you some of our newest offerings." Andrew led the two of them to a display case holding several bowls of assorted foods. "This is our latest." He offered one of the bowls and a disposable wooden spoon such as one would use to eat ice cream.

Marquaid sampled it cautiously.   "Applesauce.   With cinnamon."

"Actually that is mashed sea weed," Andrew said proudly.

"Indeed!"   Marquaid was clearly surprised.   "The taste and texture are flawless!"

"World Wide Flavors began by perfecting artificial flavorings." Andrew was proud of their accomplishments, and it showed in his words.   "Finding alternatives to expensive natural flavors used to be a hit-and-miss affair. My research led us to understand how the sense of taste works.   From that knowledge, as you see, we can exactly duplicate any taste one may desire."

The Reverend sampled the faux applesauce again. "Remarkable! And it remains fresh even in this *infernal* heat?"

An *odd* thing for a clergyman to say, although it was true enough. New York City in October *was* an inferno. Andrew was distracted by his turn of phrase.   "Ah...yes.   As you noted, the temperature is *beastly*.   Odd that it would be so warm in this supposed 'atom winter'."

"That has been part of the problem," Marquaid grumbled. "All those atom weapons made a fine hash of the weather.   The dust clouds, you know; completely disrupted the thermosphere. There's no telling from one week to the next what it'll be like.   Is it any wonder the world is wracked with famine?"   He seemed remarkably well versed in the science of the world's current woes. "But you were saying about this apple sauce?"

"Oh... Ah...that sample was made yesterday, and can remain at room temperature for as long as a week, due to the use of preservatives."

"Most remarkable, indeed!"   Marquaid sampled again, then returned the bowl to its shelf.   "But can you tell me about your artificial meats, sir? That is the heart of my purpose here."

Andrew was warming to his task now, as this new development was very much his brainchild.   "As you know, with the present adverse economic and weather conditions, the cost and availability of even basic foodstuffs has become a serious problem.   Even when food is available, a great many people cannot even afford the basics, much less such luxuries as meat."

"I am painfully aware of it, sir. Were it not for the local fishing industry where I live, many people would starve."

There was another curious note. Andrew wondered idly where his home might be. Somewhere in the Caribbean, perhaps? South America? That might explain the accent.

No matter. "We are now working to develop artificial meats using plant detritus such as corn stalks and tree leaves. We hope to provide inexpensive meat alternatives indistinguishable from the real thing in texture, color, smell, and taste." he indicated the applesauce bowl with a curt nod.

"Marvelous! But what about refrigeration? How long can your artificial meats remain fresh?"

"We anticipate that we can gain a shelf life of up to a month through the use of preservatives; far longer if they are canned or frozen."

Marquaid pondered for a moment, nodding thoughtfully. "Yes. That would solve a major problem we anticipated..." There was a faint noise from beyond Andrew's office door. Marquaid reacted as if he was stung, spinning in place, wire tense, scanning the room for danger.

"Are you all right, Reverend?" Andrew was startled and alarmed by his guest's reaction.

It took Marquaid a moment to respond, and he needed to tear himself away from the door with some effort. "Yes...sorry. One develops certain...instincts in the jungle."

Odd that his native companion hadn't so much as twitched. "I can assure you you are perfectly safe here. If there should be a problem, we have a cop on his beat right out in front."

"Um...yes, thank you." Marquaid certainly didn't seem convinced. His panicky reaction left Andrew wondering if something was off about this Reverend?

But to business: Andrew turned to the display and took down another bowl. "Another sample, sir."

Marquaid took a piece and ate it less hesitantly than before. "Bacon," he mumbled at last, still chewing. "The flavor is bang-on, but the texture is rather odd. Not bad, mind you, but one can still tell it's artificial."

74

"You see we have a way to go yet. Soft foods can be easily duplicated, but we are still working to duplicate foods with fiber or texture such as meats."

"Indeed!" Marquaid was clearly impressed. "And how soon do you suppose you will perfect your artificial meat?"

'So we come to the nitty-gritty,' Andrew thought, bitterly. So much potential, wanting only the means.

"Come, sir." Marquaid said softly. "We are well aware of your company's financial problems. These times are difficult, and there is no shame in owning to it."

In a way, it was a load off Andrew's chest. "That's true enough," he admitted. "Honestly, we are in need of a benefactor." He looked Marquaid in the eye, expressing himself man to man, as he instinctively knew he must. "I gather from your questions that you are considering the possibility?"

"We are," Marquaid replied promptly. "We wish you to develop an artificial human meat, and we are prepared to fund you handsomely." At this, his silent native companion, who watched him all the while with the deadly regard of a tiger, offered the faintest hint of a smile.

For the longest moment, Andrew was uncertain of just what he heard. Then he refused to believe he heard it. "Ah...forgive me, sir...but did you say...human...meat?"

"I did," Marquaid replied with perfect self-confidence. "You see, my companion, Onobulu, represents the Henoro tribes of the Brazilian Amazon. They are cannibals: which is common, in fact, throughout the region, not to mention in Africa, Southern Asia and the Pacific."

Human meat? What a monstrous notion! Suddenly Andrew's doubts about this 'Reverend' Marquaid exploded into genuine suspicion...

"Needless to say, the Europeans have tried for centuries to suppress their...ah...dietary nature," Marquaid went on. "But the natives are not willing to give up their traditional meat diets, which are steeped in mysticism as much as habit, and the Europeans are not willing to bear the expense of providing alternate meat sources."

Where did he hear that name before? It was right in the back of his mind...

"Our backers feel that if an inexpensive artificial human meat can be provided, it will placate the natives and gradually weaken their resistance to the European colonial powers. As they become more passive, we can encourage the Europeans to relax their control in turn, improving the natives' lot in life."

Andrew was utterly flabbergasted. "I...I...I hardly know what to say!" He sank into his chair in dismay.

"It can be done?"

"Um...well, yes, I suppose.   But what you suggest is monstrous!"

"Why?   They would actually be eating corn stalks, no?" Marquaid resumed his seat and his silent native took station by his side again, glowering at Andrew with ominous black eyes.

"But...if anyone found out...if the press were to learn of it...the impact could be unthinkable!"

"The unique nature of the product will be a deep, dark secret, of course. Unfortunately, as I said, the cannibal tradition is steeped in mysticism, and no other meat will serve. That detail will be a private matter strictly between us, and as far as the world will know, we will be giving them artificial beefsteak."

This *'Reverend'* Marquaid was the coolest customer Andrew could ever imagine. To suggest something so radical, so bizarre, and so casually!

"This is precisely why we came to you instead of developing this ourselves. We could license your discoveries, of course, but it will be less conspicuous if a small company perfects this than if...our high profile backers do."   Marquaid offered Andrew a conspiratorial wink. "This is a matter which perhaps should not attract too much interest."

"I should say so! Can you *imagine* the scandal? What you propose is explosive!"

"Indeed it is!   Think of it as an incentive to keep our relationship confidential."

Something about all this struck Andrew as very wrong. Reverend Marquaid's story...if he was in fact a priest...was plausible enough on the surface, but Andrew was convinced this mysterious benefactor had some ulterior motive. But what was it?

"Well...ah...even if we assume it can be done," he temporized, suddenly not so thrilled with the idea of this *'Reverend'* Marquaid and his backers. "There is the matter of cost. Perfecting artificial meat of any flavor will be expensive."

"Rest assured, sir, money will be no problem if we can reach an agreement on goals. The World Humanity League is strongly backed by certain patriotic organizations and individuals which are concerned about European imperialism. Funding is not an issue."

"Ah hah!" Andrew was relieved that Marquaid had unmasked himself at last. "You will forgive me, sir, but it seems you have an ulterior motive in all this. I think a greater candor is in order!"

Marquaid chuckled. "I was wondering. You're right, of course. That story about pacifying the natives is for public consumption. Our real reasons are more pragmatic: and as a part of our little conspiracy, I suppose you need to know."

Conspiracy? So this *'Reverend'* Marquaid *was* up to no good!

"Europe is in ruins following the recent conflict, and their empires are hanging on by a thread. By pacifying the natives through an alternative meat supply, we figure the Europeans will gradually withdraw their resources which are so badly needed at home. Eventually, their colonial presence will be so weakened that the native people can overthrow them...with a bit of help...thus bringing the Age of Imperialism to a long overdue end."

That phrase rang a bell in Andrew's mind. The mystery of this *'Reverend'* Marquaid had been bothering him, and now the missing piece dropped into place. It was all beginning to make sense. The Imperial Age was now largely in the past, as the Imperial powers mostly lay in ruins after the Great War of 1905-06. Andrew could see this *'Reverend'* Marquaid intended to profit from the catastrophe.

"You are a revolutionary, sir!"

If Marquaid was distressed at his accusation, he gave hardly a hint of it. "Concern about Imperialism is felt in many places and by many people," he answered briskly. "We merely do our humble part to make this a better world. But it is of no concern. What matters is that the World Humanity League is prepared to provide you with massive research funding and product orders, enough to assure your company will become a giant in the food industry."

"We want no part in revolution, sir! What you offer is unacceptable!"

Marquaid was on his feet, leaning on Andrew's desk, towering over him. "You will want to consider your options carefully," he snarled. "Our backers are *powerful* individuals who could be very *good* friends to a small and struggling company such as yours."

"N-n-no..." Andrew was shaken by his sudden menace. "...W-we can't...!"

"You are deeply in debt, and your creditors have been *most* forbearing. If your accounts were called, it would force you into liquidation. No doubt competent scientists could duplicate your efforts from studying your research!" Marquaid drilled Andrew with his cold, gray eyes. "Being in our backers' good graces could spell the difference between survival...or bankruptcy."

"But how can we do this?" Andrew said as a last feeble defense. "How can we develop...to test...to taste...h-human..."

"Not a problem, sir! We can provide expert taste-testers!" At that, Marquaid's companion grinned, and Andrew could see his teeth were filed to points!

Andrew recoiled in his chair. This was too much! He was in the presence of two madmen! "...But...if anyone found out..." He was shaken at the menace of Marquaid's basilisk gaze. "...*Human meat*, sir! My God! The scandal..."

"The whole success of this venture is based on keeping *that* little detail a secret," Marquaid replied coldly. "Certainly *you* would have no reason to reveal it!"

There was a painful silence broken only by the whirring of his desk fan and the muted street noises as Andrew struggled to find some way out of this predicament. There was none. Marquaid had him by the short hairs, and clearly was not going to let loose.

"Well, sir? What say you? Will you join us? Will you make World Wide Flavors a success?"

There was no other choice.

§

Later, after *'Reverend'* Marquaid and his native companion departed, Andrew sat in his office staring numbly at the door. The first clear impression which came to mind was that he had been in the presence of an actual cannibal! He was a mild mannered, city bred, college educated product of modern society...and he wasn't sure whether this Marquaid or his savage associate terrified him more. Clearly Marquaid was no man of the cloth! Those were the icy gray eyes of a ruthless, desperate man...

Then that name, which tickled the back of his mind for some time, came to light. *Professor* Marquaid! He was one of the so-called World Scientific League, the scientist-conspirators who developed the atom weapon! No wonder he seemed so nervous! He and his co-conspirators must be the most hunted men in the world. It was their invention of the atom weapon, back in 1895, which set off an arms race, triggering the Great War which left Europe in ruins. Their *'World Scientific Conspiracy'*, as the newspapers put it, caused the death of millions, wrecked the environment triggering the disastrous famines, and blackened the name of scientists everywhere. If caught, they would doubtless be lynched on the spot.

It all began to make sense: Marquaid must be involved in some new conspiracy, and this World Humanity League must be a front for some fiendish plot of theirs. But why drag him into their scheme?

Then it struck Andrew that there was one Imperial power—America—who stayed out of the Great War, and thus emerged with even greater prominence than before. Marquaid's tale of providing artificial meat to cannibals was clearly a fantasy. Could all this be an elaborate ruse aimed at the downfall of the United States?

The pamphlet Marquaid gave him caught his eye. Curious, he picked it up and read through it. As he suspected, the League's backers were some of the most rabid nationalists at large today. Teddy Roosevelt, for one, was right at the top of the list, and Andrew recognized several other embittered imperialist demagogues, radical newspapers, and ultrapatriotic leagues. No doubt they were duped into publicly supporting this so-called World Humanity League. No doubt this Marquaid dangled his second story of weakening the European colonial powers in front of them. No doubt if the tattered remnants of the European empires collapsed, America was ideally placed to step into the vacuum. It would be a succulent lure, indeed, to men of that stripe.

Then Andrew caught it: what would happen to those who funded and endorsed the creation of such a revolting product as artificial human meat? The political consequences of exposure would be horrific! Clearly they had no idea of the true nature of this undertaking! Should their plot suddenly be exposed, *especially* in a sensational and repulsive manner, there could be little doubt as to the consequences for those ultranationalistic backers.

Andrew felt a rising tide of panic. Everything he labored so long to build was threatened! His first reaction was to raise the alarm. Marquaid couldn't have gone far in the last few minutes. The city police could surely seal off Manhattan Island, throw out a dragnet, round up the arch-conspirator and his savage companion. Then at least World Wide Flavors would be spared the scandal...

...But it would matter not. Marquaid was right: World Wide Flavors teetered on the edge of bankruptcy. Without the support of his rabid financial backers, they were doomed. If that happened, all his labors, all his genius, his many discoveries, his reputation, his life savings would be lost. In a world which viewed scientists as arch-fiends, he would have little to look forward to, indeed.

He stared at the brochure without really seeing it as he thought desperately trying to come up with an answer. One thing was certain: his inventions would be saved. The world was too hungry for his creative genius to fade away. But without him at the helm, what would become of his discoveries? More important, what would become of him? What to do?

Well, for one thing he needed to publicly separate himself from this pending shipwreck. Bannerman: of course, his friend Frank could help him. Bannerman and Green were some of the brightest legal minds on Wall Street, and not ones to scruple at a sharp deal. They could set up some sort of hidden trust; that way he, Andrew, could publicly disassociate himself from the coming storm while maintaining his interest in his creations.

His mind raced feverishly, and he sprang to his feet, pacing back and forth. This would be the perfect moment too: a buyout, with the new owners embarking on their disastrous course, and he all unaware of their *evil* intentions. Yes, it would work! He could save his reputation and his creations, and no doubt profit enough to start over. If *anyone* could profit from disaster, Frank was the man!

With that burden off his mind, he turned his thoughts to Marquaid and his World Scientific League. He recalled reading somewhere how they protested the use of their terror weapons during the Great War. To hear it said, they warned the world of the dangers their breakthrough presented. They could hardly be blamed if the world refused to listen.

Given that light, Marquaid and his associates didn't seem like such an evil lot after all. But what about this affair? They must have decided to turn to revolution, and who could blame them? Every scientist *he* knew was dedicated to making the world a better place; could they be faulted for turning bitter at how their efforts were bastardized? Be that as it may, it still left him stuck 'twixt and 'tween. Like it or not, he was caught up in their revolution...so he might as well accept the inevitable and profit from it.

He took down the bowl of faux applesauce and began nibbling absent-mindedly as he pondered the future. The apple sauce always was his favorite. It was a shame about this place. World Wide Flavors was doomed to a premature and spectacular death, but life goes on. Come to think of it, the potential profit in this revolution could be impressive; well worth the gamble. His friend Frank might take an interest too. This *'World Scientific Conspiracy'* could use some sharp legal minds. Yes, the future would be interesting indeed with this Professor Marquaid.

*****

It is a sad truth that some people simply cannot handle the temptations of even the tiniest sliver of power. We've all met the sort: officious, overbearing petty annoyances who can ruin one's day. But those who may be tempted to follow this path should be aware that such petty abuse can backfire disastrously when it collides with real *power...*

"The 8:30"

The 8:30 train was jammed that evening. The Cubs won the season opener (miracles do happen) and the westbound METRA commuter was packed with happy fans headed back to the Chicago suburbs. Normally this late train was fairly quiet, but tonight the gallery car was filled to capacity with standees in the center area; perhaps 150 people altogether, and this train had eight such cars.

§

The Conductor started his rounds as soon as they departed Chicago, working his way from front to back methodically demanding the passengers' tickets and canceling such with his hand-held ticket punch. His ticket punch, together with his classic conductor's hat and METRA badge clipped to his jacket were his tokens of authority—his emotional crutch, some would say—and he used them to the fullest.

Click-click. Click-click. He worked his punch steadily, reveling in its sound, the sound of Authority. *Click-click. Click-click.* The Man is coming.

As far as these people were concerned he was God Walking The Earth, and he made sure everyone knew it. He was a royal pain in the ass, in fact, despised by the regulars and his fellow crewmen alike, not that he cared. He was especially abrasive this evening, disregarding the half-dozen complaining letters which would inevitably follow. METRA management hassled him endlessly about it, but it did them little good. They were far away in Union Station, downtown; he was in his element, his personal empire where he ruled with an iron hand on his ticket punch and those who protested could be put down abruptly, or even put off the train if they proved too intractable.

82

Click-click. Click-click.

Yes, the world may despise him, but they didn't matter. He had his ticket punch and METRA rule book and the all-powerful Union. Let 'em scribble their pathetic letters!

Click-click. Click-click.

He was bullying his way through the third car when he came upon the perfect victim: an elderly little man, thin and frail, stylishly dressed and sporting a neat goatee. He sat alone on one of the double seats holding a large, ornate ceramic bottle.

"This car is full," the Conductor demanded. "No hogging the seats."

The little man gave him an annoyed look, but didn't move. "If anyone wishes to sit here, they are welcome to do so."

That *tone* said this runt was going to give him a fight, *just* the thing to set off his bullying instinct.

Click-click. Click-click. He worked the ticket punch restlessly, which everyone knew was a warning sign. "And there's no open liquor bottles on this train."

"It is *not* open." The little man was showing backbone. "And this is *not* a bottle; it is an amphorae."

"Yeah, I know what it is. That's one of them Roman wine bottles." He'd seen the like on a National Geographic special.

"*Grecian*, not Roman. And it no longer contains any wine."

"Yeah? What are you doing with it to begin with?"

"I am a collector of antiquities. This is a rare, I daresay unique treasure. I am transferring it to my new home in the suburbs, if you *must* know."

Click-click. Click-click.

This little worm was showing a surprising amount of spine, which stuck in the Conductor's craw. "Yeah? Well if that bottle's so valuable, why'd you bring it on the train, huh? You don't sound like no collector to me!"

Click-click. Click-click.

"Most of my collection is in the museum, downtown. A few favorite personal items are being moved by the museum staff, but this is special to me. You might say it is a personal treasure because of its unique nature."

"Unique nature, my ass! It's a cheap ol' wine bottle likely dug up from some ruins somewhere. The rules say no open liquor bottles on METRA trains, and by God, you'll obey the rules or else!"

"You don't listen so good, do you? This *amphorae* is *not* full of liquor, and it is *not* open, which any fool can see!" The little man was getting annoyed, but he was also proving a tough nut to crack, which goaded the Conductor no end.

Click-click. Click-click. Click-click. Click-click.

He wasn't used to people standing up to him like this, which left him a bit disconcerted. "So, what's so important about this-here bottle? You got a Genie in there, or somethin?"

The little man shook his head in annoyance. "There are no such things. Genies are nothing more than ancient fables."

"Well if it don't have a Genie in it, then it's got to be a wine bottle!"

"I can assure you, sir, this *'bottle'*, as you put it, is not filled with alcohol," the little man said, coldly. "If you were a *gentleman*, you would accept my word on it."

That remark struck sparks, setting off a subdued wave of approval from the crowd around them which reminded the Conductor of just how unpopular he was, which stuck in his craw. This *nobody* was undermining *his* authority, right here in *his* turf, right here on *his* train. He was being made out to look like a fool! The fact that he was doing it to himself never registered; his Godhead was being challenged—debunked!—and he wouldn't stand for it!

Click-click. Click-click. Click-click. Click-click.

"Enough of your nonsense!" The little man was getting to him. "You better prove that bottle's empty or I'll put you off this-here train!"

The little man sighed in evident annoyance. "Very well. If you insist, examine it for yourself." He held the bottle up with its neck pointed at the Conductor.

The Conductor hesitated. His bluff was being called by this ant right in front of a carload of cattle who watched in obvious amusement.

Click-click. Click-click.

Suddenly he suspected a trap was closing in on him. This shrimp was likely a railroad inspector, or perhaps some kind of civil rights legal hotdog looking to settle all those complaints which had piled up for years. He was beginning to think he was in a pickle: whether he opened the bottle or not, he was probably setting himself up for a disciplinary hearing. Worse, he would look foolish in front of these people, who were already enjoying his discomfiture.

Click-click. Click-click. Click-click. Click-click.

That made him angry. The *nerve* of these people to dispute *his* authority on *his* train! The outright *gall* of them to set a trap for *him! Click-click. Click-click.* And *this* little worm—that *must* be a fake bottle; a prop for this ambush. No one in their right mind would bring a priceless antique onto a commuter train! *Grecian* amphorae, indeed!

Click-click. Click-click. Click-click. Click-click.

His temper snapped. He grabbed the bottle out of the little man's hands and threw it down on the floor, expecting it to shatter into a million pieces. It didn't. It bounced, clattering back and forth in the narrow aisle to a chorus of protests before it finally came to rest a few feet away.

Then the stopper came loose with an eerie ringing sound, but instead of liquid, a stream of dense smoke came billowing out, coiling around the Conductor until it filled this end of the car. Momentarily startled, he was about to reprimand the little man for violating the no smoking rule. But then the cloud...*condensed...*

Whatever it was, it sure as *hell* wasn't a Genie.

Whatever it was, it was shaped like a vast worm or slug stretching half the length of the car, jammed tightly between the two rows of seats, its hideous head towering over them. Its hide was like rotted flesh, greenish-purple and blotched with corruption. Its enormous multi-faceted eyes glowed with evil fire, and its head was crowned with two leathery ears and a row of spikes running down its back. And the *smell*... The car was filled with a noxious stench of sulphur and corruption which took the breath away and left people gasping.

There was a moment of stunned silence before the passengers reacted with a chorus of terrified screams as they scrambled over the seats away from this apparition. The monster let out a bellowing roar which froze everyone in terrified paralysis. For an eternal moment nothing happened. The passengers stood or sat in frozen terror as the monster looked them over...

...then turned briefly to the little man, who gestured calmly at the Conductor. "That one," he said.

The monster glowered at him in murderous rage before turning its attention to the Conductor, who stood paralyzed before it...

...the creature emitted a deep, almost subaudible rumble which chilled the listeners to the bone...

...then its vast mouth opened slowly, revealing a forked tongue which whipped around like an agitated snake, caressing the Conductor's face and shoulders, staining his dark blue jacket, leaving a trail of greenish slime...

The Conductor's last conscious thought as he stared up into the cavernous mouth filled with row upon row of sharks' teeth was that the little man was right: there was no alcohol in the bottle. Then the creature *ate* him in six huge, slavering, ravenous gulps. The awed silence in the car was broken by a chorus of whimpers as blood and ichor splattered in all directions.

Once it finished its hideous meal, the fiend reared to full height, head spikes brushing the roof of the car, and glowered at the little man seated before it.

"Well?" He eyed the monster calmly. "You've had your sacrifice."

"What is your wish?" the creature growled.

"What?"

The fiend ground its teeth and growled at him with a hatred which was physical, like raging fire, far beyond anything mere mortals could feel. Static discharges danced among its spikes, and the car was filled with a deep, subterranean earthquake rumble as the lights flickered. They locked in frozen confrontation for a long moment, the little man replying to its hideous presence with calm regard until, finally, it was the monster which yielded. "Master!" it ground out at last.

The proprieties attended to, the little man made a brisk, sweeping gesture taking in the petrified mob. "Make all these people forget what just happened, then return to your *amphorae*. Oh, and clean up this mess." He dabbed his blood-spattered face with a dripping sleeve. "You have the *worst* table manners!"

§

The 8:30 train was jammed that evening. The Cubs won the season opener (miracles do happen) and the westbound METRA commuter was packed with happy fans headed back to the Chicago suburbs. At Naperville, a debarking passenger kicked the Conductor's ticket punch, laying unnoticed on the floor, under a seat.

*****

Far too many of us merely limp along through life, enduring the daily drudgery of a job which can be done by monkeys. We envy those who take genuine satisfaction in their work, who look forward eagerly to each new day; but career enthusiasm can be a fragile thing, all too easily shattered by an unexpected turn of events...

"It's A Dirty Job..."

"Okay, Professor Doom..."

"That's Professor *Von* Doom, thank you!"

The director gave him a sardonic look, and shrugged. "Sure. Okay, Von, we start by rolling the title credits, then we cut to the sound stage where the hosts do their monologue. Then they do the poetry segment, then the intro, and you make your entrance stage left. Got it?"

Herr Professor *Von* Doom took a deep breath to contain his rising angst. "Yes. I 'got' it."

"Marvelous, dahling. Five minutes to air time." The director spun on his heel, dismissing him without a second thought, and sashayed off to get into a hissy-fit with the cameraman.

Professor Von Doom stood in the wings of the sound stage, fists clinched, fuming over the mindless cretans who made his life an endless purgatory. Ignorant *swine!* He swore to himself that *person* in particular would be the first to feel his Righteous Wrath when he came to power. It wasn't bad enough that he had to come to these boors to carry his Ultimatum to the world; what really hurt was this obscure cable TV channel was the only outlet which had the wit to acknowledge his command. How was he supposed to conquer the world if he had to depend on *these* cretans?

§

He never expected the life of a world-conquering fascist sociopath to be easy, but this was only the latest in an *endless* stream of indignities and dismissal which dogged his path over the last two decades. These people didn't fear him, and they sure as *hell* didn't respect him! No one took his twisted genius or his world-conquering ambition seriously, but *that* was about to change.

88

His greatest invention could unleash limitless power upon his enemies, sweeping away armies, fleets, whole cities until they acknowledged his genius and bowed down before him!

But for that to happen he needed to deliver his Ultimatum to the world, and for *that* he needed the news media. And there is where an unfeeling, callous, ignorant, boorish...there was where the world threw another monkey wrench into his bold vision of the future. He sent out *hundreds* of media packets outlining his great creation (being careful not to give out too much detail) and demanding air time to make an 'announcement', then settled back to await the inevitable firestorm his commands would produce.

Dead silence.

Nothing. No response. Nought in his mailbox but grocery fliers and throwaway religious tracts. No phone calls. No reporters. Nada, day after day while his frustration built and he became steadily more unhinged. He was about ready to turn his invention loose on New York City—they'd listen to him then!—when a single letter turned up weeks later inviting him to appear on their show. It was from a cable TV channel, and in the undesirable mid-day slot, but it was a beginning.

At first glance, the show's name, 'Purple Apocalypse', sounded promising, but the more he saw of this 'cable TV channel', the less impressed he was. The show originated from a ratty, run down row house in a ratty, run down part of Queens were the walls were covered with lurid graffiti and gang sign, and derelicts sprawled on the sidewalk.

The building interior was no more promising. The wall decor was vari-colored plastic trash bags, radiation and biohazard signs, and furnishings which must have come from the alley behind a thrift store. Right opposite the main (only) entrance was a screaming poster for the Weed Rebellion, overlaid by smaller signs for Earth Day, Amnesty International, and Che Guevara.

The receptionist was a—*person*—of indeterminate age, gender, and even species, dressed in a tattered sequined ball gown, wooly sweater, high-top sneakers, and makeup which must have been applied with a mop. "Can I help you, hon?"

"Ah...I am here to appear on the 'Purple Apocalypse' program."

He/she/it/? gestured over his/her/its/?s shoulder with a feather-tipped ball point pen. "Sound studio's on the second floor. Watch out for that stair rail, it isn't safe."

"Thank you."

"Love the getup!" he/she/it/? gushed. "Black is so 'in' right now. And that cape! It's *so* retro!"

"Indeed," he said, evenly. "I daresay black will become more popular in the near future."

"You know it, sweetie!" Von Doom dismissed that overly familiar apparition, tugged his cape tighter to ward off the *unclean* sensation, and headed for the stairs. "And be sure to jiggle the toilet when you're through, love. We have the most *outrageous* water bills!"

The second floor sound stage was another shock: painted solid, bilious purple, with a row of toilets for seats, all lit by a rack of overhead lights shrouded in large coffee cans. Around the edges of the room were various broken-down sets, one of which was emblazoned 'The Truth You Weren't Meant To Hear' A single video camera was manned by a refugee from the 60s, while the director's control board was a folding table with a jumble of electronics festooned with cables. A couple more bizarre characters hung around in odd corners, although he couldn't tell if any of them were his hosts. It was about as far from his preconceived notions of a sound studio as could be. This wasn't promising: he didn't watch television, but even he could see these people were from the farthest far-outest fringes.

§

"You're Professor Doom, ain't ya?"

He was dragged out of his woeful reverie by two people who'd come up the stairs behind him. "That's Professor *Von* Doom, thank you!"

"Cool." *He* was dressed in blue jeans, a muscle shirt, and combat boots. His hair was shaved back into a bilious purple-orange spiked Mohawk, and he had rings in his lips and nose. *She* was all in black; torn hose, tattered leotard, a biker vest, and heavy Goth boots buckled up to her knees. She had Zodiac tattoos on her cheeks, and her hair and nails were dyed a sickly chemical green.

90

"Um...you are...?"

"We're the hosts of the show," he said. "Moonwolf and Sunflower, at yer service."

"Ah...yes, mister Moonwolf..."

"I'm Sunflower, she's Moonwolf."

"Oh, wow!" she gushed. "Are you really a mad scientist? That's totally awesome!"

Von Doom bit back his growing rage with an effort. "There are those who call me mad...cretinous fools! Little do they understand. My genius will topple their petty empires! I will serve notice this day that the world will submit to me or feel my wrath!"

"Man, that is like *totally* deep," the host sighed. "You're really gonna off the system?"

"There will be a new world, made in a better image.

"Jeez...no more corporate fascists?" she gushed. "No more corrupt politicians? No more Jesus Freaks tellin' us what we can't do with our own bods? You got my vote!"

"It...is not a question of votes..."

"Damn straight!" he said, emphatically. "No more parties! Power to the people!"

"Okay loves!" the director interrupted. "One minute to air. Let's shake that booty."

"That's our cue," she gushed. She did all the time, it seemed. "See ya!" They scampered on set and flopped in their places, leaving him to wonder what the *hell* he'd gotten into.

There was some last second scurrying back and forth, the lights came up, and the camera...person...focussed in. "Five seconds," the director said from his station at the equipment table. "Four...three...two...one...roll 'em!"

There was an ear-splitting blast of noise. Von Doom recoiled at the racket before he realized it was an Acid Rock riff, reverbed and amped to painful intensity. *This* was the show's theme music? Then a stern voice came in loud enough to carry over the volume: "And now, it's time for the *PURPLE APOCALYPSE!*"

With that, the racket cut off abruptly, leaving his ears ringing, so the hosts were into their dialogue before he could make much of it out. As is, he could only catch a few disjointed phrases so stilted in PC-speak that it was hard to follow the syntax. He did pick up on "Wall Street criminals" and "political whores" and "Military-Industrial conspiracy", with due reference to the FBI, and a rather incoherent relating of the CIA to the Mafia so embedded in gibberish that his much-abused ears could hardly follow it.

It appeared these people had a rabid hatred for the System and everything related to it. Normally Von Doom would share that sentiment, but now he was struck with reservations. Like them, he wanted whole-heartedly to 'off the ruling conspiracy', and like them, he intended to take it over and put it to his own purposes. The fact that these people concurred with his desires, however different their goals, was...disturbing. He thought of himself as a revolutionary iconoclast, not a...hippy! For the first time in twenty years, he began to doubt what he was planning.

§

The monologue ended, and they cut away for a prerecorded commercial from a local head shop. While this was going on, Von Doom realized someone had come up the stairs behind him. The newcomer was a heavyset man dressed in coveralls, a denim work shirt and boots. He was carrying a heavy toolbox, and seemed shockingly normal by the standards around here.

"Damn plumbin' in dis-here dump is hopeless," he grumbled. "They ought-a tear dis whole block down." He sized Von Doom up with a jaundiced look. "Dat toilet's workin' again, which ought to count as a miracle fer my Sainthood. Who do I go to with my bill *this* time?"

"I have no idea. You might try that...person...downstairs."

"*Dat* one, huh?" He shivered all over. "Da things I do t' make a living!"

The commercial ended, and they stood quietly for a bit watching as the host recited a lurid poem equating a rutabaga to a newborn infant. "Quite a spectacle, ain't it?"

"It...doesn't inspire."

"Yeah. The only thing keeps dis place goin' is they're part of a cable programming package. Only da freaks tune in on 'em." The plumber looked him up and down skeptically. "You look t' be right at home with 'em."

"Hardly! They serve my purposes for now, but I fully intend to move on to bigger and better things."

"Yeah?   Well if ya need any plumbin' gimme a call."   He produced a business card. "I make house calls anywhere, even in Transylvania."

§

The poetry segment rounded out with her raving a rabid free verse screed equating freeways to nuclear war. The effort left her drained, and she sagged on her toilet while another commercial for a Green Party candidate ran.

"You were great, Moon," the host said to her.

"Yeah. That one's got real heart, ya know?"

"I know it, babe!"

She threw an annoyed glare at him. "Watch the sexism, huh?"

The commercial ended, and they turned their attention to him. "And now, it's time for our feature segment." The host gestured toward Von Doom, waiting uneasily off camera. "Today we have a special guest, the one we've all waited *years* for. Here's the dude who's gonna lay it down to The Man, who promises to off the system once and for all, to bring back the Age Of Aquarius...let's give a big welcome to our own Mad Scientist, Professor Doom!"

There was a burst of canned applause, which the host and hostess pretended to share in. Von Doom was caught off guard, and had to shake off his bemused state before he marched onto the set, regretting all the while that he hadn't simply vaporized New York City whether it would get the media's attention or not.

Toilets are no substitute for a couch, not that he expected better at this late date. He had to resist the habit—the mortal temptation —to drop his trousers before he sat, and watched uneasily as the host started the ball rolling by providing an intro which would embarrass a plaster saint. His rant went on for several minutes as he worked himself up into the most overblown screed yet, while she gushed empty enthusiasms and anatomically improbable suggestions about prominent figures in the news.

Finally the host ran out of expletives, and turned to him. "Okay, Professor Doom..."

"That's Professor *Von* Doom, thank you!"

93

The host gave him a sardonic look, and shrugged. "Sure. Okay, Von, tell us about this ultimate power you've invented."

Something in him finally clicked. This was simply too much! Determined as he was, there were limits to what even Von Doom could, or would, endure for his cherished plans for world conquest. It sickened him to think these *creatures* whole-heartedly *approved* of his plans, and *applauded* his intent to topple the governments of the world. He spent the last *twenty years* working his evil genius to the bone for *them?*

If any two things distinguish a sociopath from lesser mortals, those are obsessive-compulsiveness and contempt for their fellow humans, and Von Doom prided himself on having both traits to the *nth* degree. He was revolted to think these mere *people* approved of and supported his fiendish plans! They may be the *fringe-de-la-fringe*, but they had an audience, and advertisers, so clearly there were others of similar ilk out there. And now that he thought about it, he recalled how *many* people from all walks of life were fed up with the System, and wanted the Powers That Be toppled. He long cherished that factoid as motivation for his fiendish plans, but his experience here put a whole new spin on that...was he playing into *their* hands? Why, by God, he might wind up with a following! Popular acclaim? The talk show circuit? The cover of Rolling Stone! A cult!

He was sickened by the thought that all his labors, his twisted genius, might amount to nothing. It was plain he couldn't go ahead with his monstrous plot now, not if the common herd approved of it...would benefit from it...applaud it...*lionize* him for it! But as much as his contempt for the herd discouraged his original plans, his obsessive-compulsiveness wouldn't let him simply give up and walk away. And he *was* a mad scientist, after all...

He sat thinking furiously as the seconds ticked away, trying to come up with an alternative...yes...of course! His twisted, Machiavellian genius came through when it was needed most. He'd show them!

"Ah...yes. My invention." He sat up a bit straighter and addressed the hosts as a reasonable man would. "I, um, have developed a source of tremendous power, an energy source which

94

uses common materials for both construction and fuel." He made a point of keeping his tone calm and civil, much to the host's obvious disappointment. "The generator for this source is fairly simple to build, so even less advanced countries can produce the units. And while they may be expense to build, the savings in energy costs will pay for them in short order. They can be made to any size desired, so can be...ah...custom tailored to meet any commercial or industrial need."

His hosts were fidgeting and throwing sidelong glances at each other. Good: they realized this wasn't going where they expected, which goaded him on in his *revised* fiendish plot.

"This process promises a new dawn of *unlimited* energy for commercial, industrial, and *military* uses. I propose to license this technology to industries and governments around the world as soon as the patent rights can be finalized."

That must have appalled both of them, if their expressions revealed anything. Great! He was on a roll, reveling in his devious evil.

"Having an unlimited source of industrial power will allow us to reserve oil, coal, and gas use for transportation. And while the process does generate waste products, they aren't that much different from nuclear reactor waste, so existing methods can be used for cleanup."

His hosts flinched at that one, both looking genuinely distressed, which fueled his rage. "I expect licensing to begin on a world-wide basis shortly. This discovery is too important, too fundamental to the betterment of mankind to limit it to any one country."

Yes! His evil genius would triumph after all! Instead of conquering the earth, he'd *buy* it!

*****

Who doesn't enjoy a lively conversation? To reach out to kindred souls, discuss professional issues, express our innermost hopes and aspirations, argue the latest ball game are our unique blessing and gift. Or are they...?

"On Language, And The Illuminati Revealed"

Since Homo Sapiens first came on the scene, we have known —known, mind you—that we are the ultimate goal of evolution. We blithely assume, since we are the only ones who build factories, automobiles, atom bombs, etc, that we are the one, the only, the true intelligent species on this world. But this comforting delusion falls apart when you realize we may have been using the wrong criteria all along. Suppose an intelligent race did not feel the need for air conditioning or the latest offerings of Hollywood? Would we even recognize them as neighbors in our cozy little country club niche of the animal kingdom?

§

Many animals exhibit behavior suggesting a reasoning intellect. Dolphins, for example, can recognize a drowning human and take appropriate action. Chimpanzees both make and use simple tools, and engage in organized warfare. Many species act together to protect their young. All of these require comprehension, decision, and concerted action by individuals for a common goal—intelligent behavior.

If any one phenomenon defines intelligence, it is the use of some means of communication: the many forms of which can be lumped under the broad category of language. You have to be able to communicate in order to convey thought, plan, and coordinate. However, many life forms communicate by non-verbal means. Gorillas have been taught deaf-mute sign language, and can engage in simple conversations. Cuttlefish flash color patterns. Bees report the location of flowers by intricate dance. Many species attract mates by releasing hormones. Even we humans use body language more than we realize. As we see from the above, a language does not have to consist of sounds or printed images.

§

The next question, of course, is what is a language? A language is a group of symbols—graphic or verbal in our case, color patterns for the cuttlefish—each symbol expressing a commonly shared concept. Express that symbol, and you pass the concept one to the next. These symbols are made up of elements —the shape of a letter, a tone of voice—variables which distinguish one symbol from another. 'A' is not 'Z'. Whispering is not shouting. Red is not green. A symbol might represent a complete concept (such as Chinese pictographs), or a speech sound used in combination to create words, as in English.

The earliest forms of Chinese pictographic language had some 50,000 concept symbols. The more refined modern forms have as few as 1,500. However, most modern Chinese terms are made of two pictograms, so those 1,500 symbols, combined in pairs, generate as many as 2,250,000 concepts.

English, by comparison, has a mere 26 symbols, plus punctuation, representing vocalizations. But these symbols can be combined in unlimited strings to create concepts ranging from 'I' to:

'contraneoquasiantidisestablishmentarianismistically'

All animals have a language, even if it is limited to a few simple concepts (food/mate/danger). Even simple animal languages require some analytical brain power, and advanced languages make great demands on the old gray matter. So a rule of thumb (if you have thumbs) is to look for a sophisticated language as the key to identifying intellectual beings. The trick, however, is recognizing a language when you see it.

§

Case in point: anyone who has been owned by a cat knows they are intelligent. Cats have a unique ability to interact with and manipulate humans. Could this be because they are *so* intelligent they have us figured, and know how to push our buttons? As much as humans like cats, our fixation with being 'the chosen' blinds us to competition for the top of the food chain. We persist in thinking cats are 'very smart, for dumb animals'.

Not that they object. Apparently belly rubs and Tuna Surprise offset lack of respect from mere humans. If they are intelligent, they are certainly capable of controlling us without revealing their secret. Take their habit of lying on your computer keyboard while you are trying to work: could they be telling you they resent your lack of attention? They rub against your legs to get you to feed them. And they purr to express satisfaction, which they know gives you gratification. Are these simple animal behaviors, or the cunning ploys of intellects vast, cool and unsympathetic?

But all the above are body language, and body language can only express a few obvious basics. If cats are intelligent, they will certainly have a sophisticated language. But cats' verbal ability is only par for the animal norm, so the real cat language, like those of bees and cuttlefish, may well be nonverbal.

As said earlier, if a non-verbal intellect spoke to us, would we recognize it? In this case, there is one possibility. We've all seen it; all witnessed cats expressing it; but our response, in our ignorance, has been disgust. Has anyone stopped to consider that hairballs might be the cats' true means of communication?

"Aw, now wait a minute!" says you. "Hairballs? How can a glop of guck be a language?"

True, a hairball, in itself, is capable of no more than a single 'bit' of binary data: hairball-no hairball; one-zero. But recall our earlier examination of language forms, and that "glob of guck" takes on ominous implications. Remember: a language is a set of symbols we call 'letters' made up of various elements which define those 'letters'. Could cats provide their own concept elements, thus increasing the data capacity of that "glob of guck"? Unconvinced? Consider some of our circumstantial factors:

A temporal factor? Alarm clock. Check.
Frequency? Political campaign advertising. Check.
Location? Kings sit above the subjects' eye level. Check.
Emphasis? Boss ripping you for being late. Check.
Size? Refer to the current issue of Playboy. Check.
Odor? Chanel #5 / sweaty gym gear. Check.
Pace? Acid Rock / Church Choir. Check.

All of these factors, as odd as they may seem, yield concept elements: the King's high throne asserting authority, for example. These elements, and others, can increase the hairball's symbolic data load.   Ponder the implications of that as we examine this factor loading further:

Time
Frequency
Location
Emphasis
Size
Odor
Pace

Assume ten element variables to each factor and array them in a seven-dimensional grid representing all the combinations:

$$T \times F \times L \times E \times S \times O \times P = \textbf{10,000,000}.$$

In other words, given ten times ten times ten times ten times ten times ten times ten element variables, each 'hairball' could carry a data load of *ten million symbols*.   Worse: 'hairball' is not limited to seven factors, or ten variables for each factor.   There may, for example, be a thermal factor, or color, or density, or time-since-deposit; or more subtle factors such as magnetic orientation, or weather interactions, or trace elements, or radioactive decay rates, and we all know cats can find a hundred places to barf.

$$T \times F \times L \times E \times S \times O \times P \times ? \times ? \times ...$$

'Hairball' is a nonhuman creation, which makes it difficult for us to recognize, much less comprehend, but as a language it clearly leaves any human dialect in the dirt.   Does Kitty rolph in your shoe / in the morning / while you're in the bathroom?   Assume Kitty is intelligent: what is she saying?   Does Tom heave on your recliner / when its raining / between 8 and 10 PM?   Assume Tom is intelligent: what is he telling you?

Time x Frequency x Location x Emphasis x Size x Odor x Pace x what else? The potential is mind-bogging.

§

No human knows the full depth and subtlety of 'hairball', but we can see that a reasonable array of factors could produce so *many* symbols that cats' intellect would have to be truly cosmic to conceive and use it. In point of order, moreover, cats usually only deliver one 'hairball' at a time, so we can only surmise they assign a complete topic to each symbolic combination: like Chinese pictographs, but each an entire book.

One thing is clear: those gooey messes we so blithely wipe up with a paper towel and throw in the garbage could be vast storehouses of subtle wisdom. For all we know, each 'hairball' could be a novel, a philosophical discourse, a groundbreaking scientific paper. Imagine it: an endless array of linguistic variables, distilled into one glop of hair. 'Gone With The Wind' wrapped in a kleenex. It puts the latest and greatest of our laughable so-called information technology into the same category as spray painting the outline of your hand on the wall of a cave. Twenty-six letters? Yeah, right.

§

So *are* cats intelligent, the true 'chosen'? You would certainly think so from how they treat us: demanding, indulgent, imperial, aloof; like any master. Here lies the true horror of 'hairball', and a revelation which will shake our world and our faith in ourselves.

It would take a vast intellect to master a language like 'hairball', and from the evidence we've seen, cats have it. Cats appear to be far more intelligent than we; far more sophisticated; expressing their genius in a language we can barely comprehend. Truly, *they* appear to be 'the chosen'.

So where do we humans come into the picture? Nature is ruthless: the strong dominate the weak. Despite our presumptions, this applies to us, as well. Our supposed 'pets' may well have relegated the drudgery of building cities and cultivating food to these also-ran humans while 'They' reign over us like Mandarin Oligarchs from the comfort of the sofa. For all we know, the phrase 'owned by a cat' is grim reality.

And here lies the danger: for we *do not* know. We assume cats are just 'clever animals' whose safety and well-being are an indulgence. *But what if we're wrong?*

In ancient times, cats were worshipped. The Egyptians built palaces for them. They had human slaves, and dined on rare delicacies. Dead cats were mummified and enclosed in royal tombs. Maybe those ancient Pharaohs knew something? Life certainly hasn't been so good for cats since. While They are popular pets, They are not worshipped as of old, and the lot of many cats is not enviable.

Look at all the hungry, homeless strays. Think of all the road kills. Ponder all the unwanted cats 'put to sleep'. And brood, if you will, over all the cats who are spayed and neutered. No doubt They do. And like all Oligarchs, They would tolerate our existence only for Their convenience. What will happen when They decide the Humane Society death camps outweigh your can opener? Is it possible that hairball you just cleaned up was a final manifesto to clean up *our* act...or suffer the consequences?

So next time you see a homeless stray being sick in the alley behind your condo, put out some cat food, or better yet, some caviar. The alternative is too grim to ignore.

*****

Reality is a snare and a delusion, so the mystics would tell us. That's a prophecy easily dismissed. Reality is all around us; touch it, does it not exist? It's easy to scoff at those who claim Divine Revelation...but what if they actually know something...?

"On The Street Of Dreams"

"Repent! Sinners! Judgment is upon you!"

You see a hundred like him on the streets of New York City: scrawny, ragged, matted filthy hair and beard, dressed in a crude approximation of biblical robes—in this case a sheet with a hole in the center duct-taped at the waist, and rubber shower tongs. The sight both annoyed and chilled David Harrison. A cheap sheet from a thrift store? In this weather? He never was long on empathy, except when it came to sniffing out a deal, but the thought was enough to give him the shivers. This guy was off his meds, big time.

"Sinners!" The ragged vagabond waved his sign and screamed at the holiday passers-by who studiously ignored him while passing as far from him as the sidewalks allowed. "The End is nigh! The doomed shall know the face of darkness!"

"Darling, we'll miss our train." Angela tugged at his arm in vexation.

Yeah, right. That set David fuming again. Spending the holiday with the relatives in Connecticut was her idea. He didn't care for her family, her mother in particular. They just didn't grasp what it means to be on Wall Street. By God, he walked among the Lords of Creation, albeit as a junior player; they were middle management: peasants.

"Sinners! Judgment is upon you! Repent!"

These encounters were uncomfortable for all concerned, but Angela was determined to trot her Wall Street stud in front of her family at every opportunity. So after surviving the weather and the holiday traffic, they were right across the street from Grand Central Station. But getting across that street without becoming New York roadkill would be a neat trick.

Two taxis were stranded in the middle of the intersection after a minor fender-bender. The cabbies waved their arms and argued in Farsi or Hindi or some-such jabber while the traffic squeezed past around them. The streets were backed up in all directions as hordes of taxis, limos, and the occasional city bus tried to connive or bully their way through the log jam. The din of horns and revving engines was deafening, and the oily stench of exhaust was giving him a headache. The taxi drivers were the worst: frustrated suicide bombers, clawing their way through by sheer intimidation. Getting across this last street would take luck more than anything else.

"This is pathetic," David grumbled. If this was how his weekend was starting out, the rest of it would be sheer hell. Angela hated her parents almost as much as he did, and grabbed every excuse to rub their noses in it. The same went for her former classmates at that jerkwater college, and even the neighbors. She'd married up, and made sure everyone knew it.

"Sinners! Bow down to the Creator! The hour is upon you!" And on top of *everything* else, here was that ragged fool and his sign. Enough is enough. David gauged the traffic, an opening appeared, and he made a tentative move...a taxi swerved past, practically on the sidewalk, splashing icy slush over his trousers.

"God...!" he gasped. "*Dammit!*" This was *just* too much. He shook his legs futilely, trying to shake off the muck and road salt running down into his shoes. These were his new Guccis! His angst boiled over, and he did the Frustration Tango, looking around at random for some indefinable release...

"Sinners!" The sign waved frantically back and forth, all but hitting him in the face. "Pray now! Judgment is nigh! The doomed shall know the face of Darkness!"

"Can't you get rid of all these damned cars?" David growled. That was just a reflexive gripe—Heaven forbid he be seen chatting with street sweepings—and he really didn't expect a reply. But the ragged creature stopped, and turned, and stared at him—or rather through him. *'Shit, got a crazy one here.'* David was suddenly worried: for all that he was a scrawny shrimp, this guy could be dangerous.

"Uh..." the street creature mumbled at last, "...yeah, sure. I can do that."

'Probably fried his brains on drugs,' David decided. At least he didn't seem dangerous, thankfully. The whole thing was so improbable that his ill mood faded, and he was momentarily amused by this pathetic cretin.

"Darling, we really have to be going." Angela tugged at his arm and eyed the street prophet with obvious distaste. Blue-blood wannabee: she still didn't grasp she was just eye candy to advance his career. That, and an adequate lay.

"Hold your horses," he rebuked her. "We'll catch the next train if we have to." He ignored her pout and turned back to the vagabond, intent on a bit of sadistic distraction. "Well, then, why don't you?"

The street prophet stared through him for another long moment, as if forming a simple thought meant marshaling all his remaining mental facilities. "Um...'cause you gotta say 'please'," he mumbled at last. "S'pos t' say please an' thank you."

This was ludicrous. David was so tickled by the whole bizarre scene that trains and taxis and dripping guck were forgotten. "You're right, actually," he chuckled. "So will you *please* get rid of all these cars?" He ignored Angela's ill-tempered tug, and waved his free arm at the thundering herd fighting its way past. "We have a train to catch."

Again the ragged messiah stared through him at some infinitely distant horizon. "Huh? Ah...sure," he mumbled at last. "Here, hold this."

Before he realized it, David found himself holding the street prophet's sign: a broomstick with a big piece of cardboard duct-taped to it, with THE END IS NEAR scrawled in crude block letters. And the fool was tottering down the street, leaving *him* to look like a prize chump.

'Probably headed back to the shelter,' David thought as he glanced around in nervous embarrassment, praying fervently that none of the senior partners would come riding by. The hypercompetitive Wall Street jungle showed no pity to the non-conformist.

"You are ridiculous, *darling,*" Angela growled in her best blue-blood wannabee sneer.

He was beginning to think she was right when the street prophet halted a dozen paces away, turned to the traffic, raised his arms in the best Cecil B. DeMille style, and let out a string of some foreign gibberish. David was momentarily bemused by the frail cretin's volume, loud enough to be heard clearly over the roar of traffic, before an unearthly glow erupted around them, swelling to fill the Universe, blinding them with its glare before disappearing again.

It took them a few seconds since they were dazed by that burst of unearthly light. Angela caught it first, and her panicky squeak alerted him. The street was empty. Up and down the Avenue as far as they could see, on the cross streets, in the taxi stand at the station: nothing.

"What the..." David gasped. The two taxi drivers looked around in astonishment, then took off in different directions, running from they knew not what. Through his shock and dismay, he understood what they felt. The next thing he realized, the street messiah had wandered back over to them.

"What...what did you do?"

"...uuuuhh?...uh...I got rid of 'em, like you asked."

"Where are they?" Angela whimpered to herself. "Where did they go?"

"...uuhh...din' go nowhere. Made 'em *not*, ya' know?"

"But...all over Manhattan?" Angela wasn't the bored blue-blood now.

"...ummm...ever'where. All of 'em, jus' like you asked."

It took David several seconds to absorb that before the implications began sinking in. *'Transportation issues will go to hell, come Monday,'* he realized. "Everywhere? All over the world?"

"...um...yeah. Like you asked."

This was *too* sweet. *'Better come in early,'* he thought. *'This'll be the ultimate insider deal!'* But then another market factor crossed his mind; one you don't normally see on the Big Board. "What about the drivers? The passengers?"

The street prophet stared, then, "...um...I made 'em *not* also. Can't have 'em hit the pavement at 60 per." He tapped the side of his head in a knowing gesture. "Total road rash, ya' know? Kinder like this."

Scratch any Wall Street killings. Hundreds of millions of people all across the country—the whole world—were suddenly *'not'*. The panic would be righteous. The economy would tank for *damned* sure.

Their eyes met, and David saw something—some unfathomable depth—which chilled him to the bone. He stared, transfixed by the emptiness in those eyes—an emptiness which drew his very soul out of him. And as his consciousness sank deeper and deeper into that emptiness, he got a glimpse of what looked back at him. Were there stars in there? He realized without comprehending that whole galaxies—an entire Universe—lay in those rummy, bloodshot eyes. Then he realized in uncomprehending horror that the seconds this ragged messiah needed to gather his thoughts, the delay he mistook for the comic struggles of a brain-damaged loser, were the reaction time of an intellect so vast, so remote, so utterly *alien* that the fate of mankind was a mere *'to do'* item.

'The doomed shall know the face of Darkness.'

"God..." He shook off the sensation, and prayed for the first time since he was a kid as the street cretin, the shell used by some unspeakable power to connect with this earth, watched silently. "All those people? Every car in the world?"

"...uh...yeah, man."

Every truck, every bus...trains? Planes? Ships? Even if it was just the cars, there were millions of them; three hundred million or more just in the USA. And it was the height of the rush hour...

"C-can you...bring them back?"

And it was his fault. He shuddered at the emptiness in those eyes; an emptiness which was finally aware of him; which hungered; which regarded him with cool disdain.

'The doomed shall know the face of Darkness.'

106

"...uh...no, man. Tha's creation. Done that gig." The messiah twitched nervously, and looked at them with a new, unnatural—unholy—presence. "Destruction's the scene now. Tha' whole Armageddon thing. Worl' gotta end some time."

"Let's GO, darling!" Angela snarled in fear as she hauled on his arm. She always was the practical one. He followed numbly, looking both ways out of habit for non-existent traffic.

"Hey, man, my sign?"

David stopped in the street, standing stupefied in a puddle for a long moment before he realized he still held the sign: broom stick, cardboard, duct tape, crude block letters spelling out THE END IS NEARER. He handed it back. "Thank you," he mumbled without willing it.

The ragged messiah stared again as his thoughts slowly gathered. "...No biggy, man. Uh...hey, you got a dollar?"

*****

Death preys upon us all. Generally we don't think of dying when we're young, but as the years pass the awareness of impending doom grows more and more to occupy our thoughts. Some fear Death; some long for it. Most are resigned to it with what good grace we can muster. And some plan to cheat Death of it's prize, which is easier said than done...

"Nothing Ventured"

"How does it look, doctor?" Webster was in a cold sweat by time the X-rays came back. "Is it lung cancer?"

Doctor Messenbaum repressed his frustrated sigh and put on his best bedside face. "No, it's not cancer. You have a common cold, is all." Webster was one of the practice's steadiest patients, and tried *his* patience to distraction at times.

"But this ache in my chest...the persistent cough..."

"Simple congestion: it's common in people your age." What he didn't say was *'You are a hypochondriac. You need to see a shrink and quit wasting my time!'* That would be impolitic with one of their best cash customers, besides which it wouldn't do any good. He used to think Webster's constant carping was self-serving pity, but had come to realize the old man's fears were sincere. He suffered all the usual minor geriatric aches common in the elderly, but let it go entirely to his head.

"But...congestion? This is too severe to be a cold! If it isn't cancer, it must be congestive heart failure!"

There are limits to the patience of a Saint, which the doctor didn't aspire to. "It's a simple chest cold! Get yourself some OTC cough syrup and go to bed. You'll feel better in a few days." Which was about how long they had until his *next* supposed life-threatening health crisis.

The desk nurse offered a good bye as he trudged out, but he ignored her. A common cold? He was vastly relieved it wasn't lung cancer or congestive heart failure...emphysema? No, the symptoms were wrong. Bronchitis? An allergic reaction? A collapsed lung?

Still, a common cold could be *dangerous*. He could develop complications, pneumonia, sinusitis, strep throat. This was far from trivial, despite the doctor's assurances. That quack didn't take this seriously; didn't even write a prescription for him. OTC cough syrup, indeed!

§

Webster spent the next week in bed, snuggled under two comforters with the heat turned up, chug-a-lugging cough syrup as if his life depended on it. Naturally the cough syrup made him groggy, naturally he sweated a river, and naturally he soon convinced himself he'd contracted malaria. His next doctor visit earned him nothing but an ill-tempered rebuff from a caregiver pushed to where he just didn't care any more.

He was physically and emotionally drained by time he got home. He trudged up the stairs in his ramshackle old house, and ground to a halt in front of the full length mirror next to the dresser. His reflection was depressed, back-sore and foot-aching, and still slightly damp. He looked and felt like old bedding slept in for a month.

"You're a sorry case, old boy," he mumbled. His hair was whiter than ever, and he noticed how *thin* it had become. "You aren't long for this world, that's for sure."

The weight of his years, of his many imagined illnesses bore him down, and for a fleeting moment he wondered if dying would be such a terrible thing? He had no family, no friends, he rarely left this old barn except for groceries and doctor visits: it wasn't like he'd be missed.

But that line of thought stoked his neurotic fears. As mean as his life was, he was *alive*, and intended to remain that way as long as possible. If only those medical cretins could figure out what was wrong with him! It was increasingly clear he couldn't count on *doctors*...but what alternatives did he have?

"Damn," he mumbled. "I'd sell my soul to be healthy again." He was being foolish, but the thought relieved some of his long-standing angst. Well why not, he wondered? It wasn't as if his soul was worth much, and if it could buy him a few aches-and-pains-free years, then it'd be worth it.

"Why not?" he muttered. "Why not sell my soul?" His angst swelled within him, and he turned and addressed the room. "Did you hear me, world?" he said aloud. "I'll sell my soul to be healthy again! To be rid of these aches and pains, these stiff joints, and the back ache, and my poor eye sight, and the stomach problems..."

"Yes, yes, I get the message!"

He spun around: the Devil was watching him from inside his mirror. "So," he said. "Are you just spouting off, or are you ready to deal?"

Webster suddenly found himself caught on the horns of a dilemma. He knew full well what sort of 'deal' the Devil had in mind, which terrified him. But against that, he was clearly dying of...*something*...and the Devil was the only one who could help him. He nodded reluctantly.

"Alright, then." The image in his mirror vanished, and he felt a strange, *unearthly* presence behind him. He spun around again, and the Devil was standing in the middle of his bedroom. He was fairly tall and agelessly handsome, with chiseled features, a gym figure, slicked-back hair and a neat goatee, dressed in oxide brown cords and loafers. The only hint of his 'devilishness' was his bright red turtleneck shirt. And the tail. "So," the Devil greeted him with a *warm* smile. "Let's play make-a-deal."

This shit was all of a sudden getting way too real! Webster edged back against the mirror in near panic. "Um...hey, maybe I was a bit hasty..."

"I know what you mean. I get that all the time, but honestly, you don't have anything to worry about. Trust me."

"T-trust you? You're the Devil!"

The Devil gave him a chilly glare. "I don't go calling you names, do I? But, hey, I know the rep, so I won't fault you. Hell isn't bad, really. You'll like it there."

"It's...hell..."

"Look, about that, we get a lot of bad press. Our competition are a bunch of conformist up-tight prigs, and they have the media sewed up solid. That hellfire-and-brimstone thing is agitprop, pure and simple. Actually hell isn't all that different than here in the mortal plane, only without the politics."

110

"It is?" (Suspiciously.)

"Trust me. We can fit you up with a cozy apartment—we've got new developments going up in the valley and the mountains, both." The Devil pondered him for a bit. "You...don't strike me as a valley guy. No matter, there's plenty of room. You can pick up an easy part-time job in a book store or some such, and I know this little coffee shop where you can do lunch. What's not to love?"

"But...what I heard..."

"The hellfire thing?" The Devil sighed. "Makes a great disincentive, doesn't it? We have more important things to do than burning you for all eternity for some stupid thing you did twenty years ago. Agitprop: nothing but made-up scandal."

"So...why do you want my soul, anyway?" (Dubiously.)

The Devil mused over his answer. "It's an economic thing. The population growth keeps the building trades busy putting up condos and shopping malls and such, plus there's the general consumer trade. It's good old fashioned demand-side economics! Immigrants fuel economic growth and bring in new vitality. We don't have recessions, trust me."

"But..."

The Devil uttered a weary sigh. "Like I said, agitprop, pure and simple. Both us and *them* are in the same market, so to speak, only our policy of granting wishes makes us a lot more popular. Hence the yellow press."

"Um...you say so." (Uncertainly.)

"I say so. Trust me. So, you know what I want; the question now is what do you want?"

There were those horns of dilemma again. As nice as the Devil made hell sound, the idea still terrified Webster. But the alternative was a few short, miserable years of deteriorating health ending in death...then inspiration slapped him up-side his head *just* when needed most. He hesitated, thinking fast; yes! It was unorthodox! Original! Brilliant! He could catch the Devil out and cheat fate itself. "I...I w-want to live forever," he stammered.

The Devil sighed. "*Another* one?"

So much for originality. "What do you mean *another one?*"

"You have no *idea* how often I get that."

"Well...even so, it's what I want. Do you want my soul or not?"

The Devil offered a placating gesture. "It's just that immortality is labor-intensive. You'd be amazed at how *stupid* some people can be when they figure they can't be killed. There are several simpler options you might want to try."

"No. I want to be immortal."

"Perhaps I can interest you in an Elixir Of Youth? It'll dial you right back to age twenty; you can start all over again."

That was tempting, mortally so, but Webster held out. "No, thank you. I want to be immortal."

The Devil frowned, which about made Webster fill his shorts. "Another fifty plus years of life is quite a gift. I can assure you most recipients figure that's plenty when the end comes."

"No, I want to be immortal! Having a new life doesn't protect me from accidents or disease."

"How about I throw in a billion dollars?"

"No."

"Ten billion?"

Tempting. "No."

"How about I make you irresistible to women as well? That and ten billion, you could party for the next half-century."

Talk about Faustian temptation! "Sorry. I'll only settle for the true deal. Immortality or nothing."

"I'll even throw in a mega-erection: enormous, iron hard, up on demand. Throw in the irresistible and ten billion, and you can *really* party."

"Sorry. Immortality or nothing."

The Devil let out a frustrated sigh. "You're a hard one," he grumbled. "Alright then: your soul for immortality. Deal?"

A belated hint of caution crept in. "Um...so when do you get my soul?"

"When you die, of course."

"But I'm supposed to be immortal! Is this a rip-off?"

The Devil greeted that with a derisive snort. "Hardly! I've been at this a lot longer than you, so I've got all the angles covered. Sooner or later you'll get tired of living and decide to give up your immortality. We'll settle accounts then."

"Um, you say so."

"I say so. Trust me. It never fails. So, is it a deal?"

Webster fought down his misgivings, which were monumental; *immortality* was staring him in the face. "Yes."

"Marvelous." The Devil considered him for a long moment. "Like I need the extra work," he muttered. Then his eyebrows crept up. "Hmm, we could give that a try," He reached into his jacket, brought something out, and tossed it to Webster. "Done!"

The object was a Rubik's Cube. "What the hell...what's this?"

The Devil gave him a sardonic look. "You've heard the expression *'Death comes for all'*?"

"Yeah?"

"That's how it works. Death will literally come for you. When he does, give that to him. He's the original obsessive-compulsive; he won't be able to put it down, so you'll be safe."

Webster pondered the cube. "You're sure this'll work?"

"Trust me: I invented them; one of my *kinkier* moments."

"Oh." Webster was still doubtful. "These haven't been around that long. Is this how you manage these things?"

"Innovation! Immortality is *so* labor intensive, so I'm always looking for better ways. My latest solution for an age-old problem: a handy-dandy labor-saving device, eh?" The Devil paused before leaving. "One note. Don't let Death touch you, that's all it takes. Toss it to him, and get the *hell* out of his way."

"Right."

§

Over the next several months, Webster became increasingly disenchanted with his great deal with the Devil. Yes, he was supposedly immortal...there was only one way to be sure...but he was still an old man plagued with his legion of ills. He cursed the Devil for tricking him: he, Webster, should know better!

Then, on somber reflection, he realized it wasn't the Devil's fault. He demanded and got immortality, but forgot to specify an end to his many ills, or to further aging. He cursed *himself* for being too eager to accept a deal. Now he was fated to get...*old*...

"I should have held out for the ten billion," he grumbled.

§

Despite his dire apprehensions, years went past. He grew older and more tired, the aches were more frequent and he slept poorly. His digestion got worse and his hair fell out until there was only a wispy fringe around his ears. His strength faded, and he spent more and more time in bed until he was effectively bedridden. He ceased going out altogether, and arranged to have his groceries delivered. He accepted it all with quiet resignation, partly because he *knew* he couldn't die, and partly because it was his own damn-fool fault for not thinking before speaking. Five years on, and he'd largely forgotten about his inevitable confrontation with Death...

...but Death hadn't forgotten him.

His first hint of trouble came on a spring day about eight years later; a faint, steady clattering sound coming from somewhere. He sat up in bed with an effort, suddenly worried, wondering what made that *ominous* noise. A moment later, the bedroom door opened, and there stood Death in all his black-robed skeletal horror.

Webster gasped in dismay as Death slowly entered the room and stopped near his bed, holding one hand out invitingly. "No!" he cried in terror. "I'm not ready!" He rolled off the far side of the bed and struggled to his feet as Death moved deliberately to head him off with a steady clattering sound of bare bones.

Then Webster remembered the Rubik's Cube. Where was it!? He'd all but forgotten about it these last few years. Where did he put it? Death was rounding the end of the bed, so he dove headlong across to the other side and scrambled in a panic-stricken rush yanking drawers open while the spectral figure came shambling after him. It wasn't in the dresser! He headed for the medicine cabinet, with Death cutting the corner to overtake him. Not there either!

He stumbled downstairs to the kitchen, gasping for breath, his heart pounding, with Death closing steadily. The cutlery drawer! The pots and pans! Death was closing in, trapping him! Not in the pantry either! In panic, he struggled over the divider into the dining room and began yanking out the drawers in the credenza, scattering their contents in utter panic. Place settings, plates, holiday decorations...Death rounded the corner and was closing with fearful speed! He ran as best he could, hobbling on his bad leg into the living room. There! The TV stand! His last chance! He dove headlong, yanked the tape drawer open...there it was!

Death was almost on him, both skeletal arms out to grab him. He scooped up the Rubik's Cube, yelled "Here!" and tossed it as Death bent over him. Death reflexively grabbed the cube...

...and stopped...

...and straightened up...

...and began fiddling with it.

Webster lay on his back, trembling, heart racing, gasping in terror as Death towered over him. He could hardly believe his eyes; it worked! The Devil was right! Death stood not two feet away, within easy reach, ignoring him as it fiddled with the cube, twisting it back and forth to the steady faint rattle of bare bones.

It took Webster a moment to overcome his panic, then he rolled over on hands and knees and crawled away, being careful not to brush the hem of Death's spectral rags. He stopped when he reached the couch and sat on the floor, shaken and bemused by what just happened. He'd beaten Death!

"I'm gonna live forever!" he wheezed in exaltation.

Death gave him a surly look, as if he was saying *'You just wait'*, then when back to fiddling with the cube.

§

The next several months became steadily more hallucinatory. Death stood in the middle of his living room fiddling with the cube, which left Webster wondering how to deal with this ultimate unwelcome guest. He found himself spending more and more time in there, watching Death from a discreet distance as he worked the cube relentlessly. He eventually started speaking to him, trying inanely to strike up a conversation. Death never answered except to give him a hate-filled glare as his boney hands worked the cube with a steady dry rattle.

Even more disturbing, he felt a growing urge to *touch* Death, to shake his hand or slap his bony face. It would mean instant death, of course. He fought the urge, and soon became convinced it was some compulsion sent by the Devil to trap him. And as time went by and that urge tormented him, he became convinced the Devil had lied to him as well. Everything he'd ever heard about hell said it was...hell. Book stores? Coffee houses? Condos? If hell was like this mortal earth, then why bother having it in the first place? It didn't make sense...not as much as a Devilish plot did. So he fought down those urges, but the atavistic instinct was always there, taunting him.

Finally, several months later, he couldn't take any more. His fear grew so great that he gave up on his living room altogether, avoided going in there, and tried to pretend it and its ghastly occupant didn't exist.

Life went on...

§

August 10, 2035 AD

It took him a while to realize the unfamiliar noise which dragged him out of a weary stupor was someone pounding on his door. "Who could that be?" he mumbled. He hadn't received visitors in *decades*. The pounding came again, which roused his suspicions. He struggled out of bed, limped cautiously down the stairs, sidled past Death who was as busy as ever with his cube, and yanked open the front door.

"Oh!" The young man on his porch was surprised by his sudden appearance. "I didn't think anyone still lived here."

"Well you thought wrong. What do you want?"

"Um, I'm from the State Survey." He produced a handful of documents, and gestured to the one he'd just nailed to the door. "I'm here to post these condemnation notices."

"*Condemnation?* You're condemning my house?"

"We have to tear down the whole neighborhood. This area is being redeveloped for senior housing."

Webster looked up and down the block and saw it was true. The street, once a bustling community, looked vacant and vandalized, and bulldozers were at work leveling the next block over. He was slightly dismayed by how the world had passed him by. "Why d'you have to tear my house down? Can't you build your senior center somewhere else?"

"Haven't you followed the news?" The young man seemed incredulous. "The senior population is exploding! It's been like

116

this for about fifteen years now. No one dies any more, so the world population is skyrocketing."

That sent a chill through him, since it didn't take a genius to see what was happening. A population explosion? No one was dying? A likely story! His suspicion blossomed into real fear. This young man must be in league with the Devil! They wanted to get him out of his house so he'd be vulnerable. "I won't go!" he said. "There's plenty of land in this area to build on."

"Not really. We need every square foot of farmland to feed the growing population, and much of the city has already been converted to senior residences."

Webster's fear amped up into paranoia. *Senior* residences? He'd heard enough horror stories about *those* places! They *must* be the work of the Devil! "Well you can't build here! This is my home, and I'm not leaving!"

After the young man went away, Webster stood in his living room trembling and breathing hard. "You won't have me," he muttered. "This isn't fair. We made a deal, and you'll live up to it, so help me!" He noticed Death watching as he fiddled endlessly with the Rubik's Cube. "D'you hear me?" he shouted. "You don't get my soul until I give it up! You tell him!"

Death didn't reply, except to give him a smoldering glare.

A week later the young man came back with a court order and four large men in white jackets. He tried to bar the door, but they forced their way in and cornered him in his living room.

"I'm sorry we have to evict you," he said as he stood right next to Death, paying no notice to him. "This project is already behind schedule. These gentlemen will take you to a senior facility."

Two of them corralled him by his arms, but must have been reluctant to get rough with him, since he was able to break free. He tried to run for the kitchen, almost stumbled into Death, and they caught him again as he frantically backpedaled. "No, you won't have me!" he wheezed at Death. "You tell him this isn't right!"

"I'm sorry about this, but there's nothing I can do," the young man said. "Don't worry. You'll like where you're going. It's a lovely place, really."

That set him off. They dragging him toward the door by his arms between them...they were dragging him right to where Death was standing! "Nnnnooooo! Not like this!" The Devil's fiendish plot was revealed! These were his minions, intent on dragging him to his doom! "Nnnnnnooooo! This isn't faiiirrrr!"

"What's with this guy?" one of them muttered as he fought them with desperate strength.

"Senile," another said. "He's gotta be over a hundred."

They struggled with him as he thrashed and whimpered in terror, reluctant to hurt him by being too forceful. "Alright," one of them said at last. "We'll take him out the side door if it makes him any happier. Bring the ambulance up the driveway."

§

The so-called Senior Facility they delivered him to was a nightmare: an enormous warehouse filled to *overflowing* with beds packed side by side. They plopped him unceremoniously on a bed in a corner. A nurse collected his name, issued him a number, and gave him a sedative. "God, how many does this make?" one of the white suits asked her.

She stared at him in bleary-eyed exhaustion for a long moment before answering. "Does it matter? The numbers just keep going up and up, and there's no end to it. I don't know where we're gonna put 'em all, much less how we can take care of 'em." There must have been ten thousand elderly people packed into that warehouse, with a hundred or so hard-pressed staff to tend to them.

"Yeah, it's hopeless," the white suit said. "It's the apocalypse. I thought we were supposed to be consumed in fire, not drown in our own sewage!"

No sooner were they through with him than he felt that familiar aura again. "So how's life these days?" the Devil asked.

"It's living hell!" he mumbled. "Why'd you drag me here?"

"Hey, this wasn't my idea! They needed your lot to build some sort of shelter."

"Huh? Those weren't your minions?"

"Nope. They thought this up all on their lonesome. I'm sorry I didn't drop by earlier to warn you, but I've been busy trying to cope with the crisis."

"What crisis?"

The Devil sighed. "Since Death got tangled up in that cube, no one's been dying. Immigration has dropped off to nothing. We're trying to stave off a full-blown recession in hell!"

"No one...? So what they said was *real?*"

"It's bad. Unemployment is climbing, the excess housing is a drag on the building trades, consumer confidence..."

"To hell with hell! What about here?"

The Devil gave him an annoyed look. "*Their* population is expanding by leaps and bounds. They're running out of room, food, everything. They're fighting over the scraps. I suppose they consider it a crisis of some sort."

"And all because of your damned cube? You idiot!"

"Granted, and you're not the first to ream my ass over it. We have to stop this now so our economy can recover."

That didn't sound good. "What d'you want from me?"

"You need to take the cube back. That way Death can go back to work."

Webster smelled a not very subtle trap. "Not a chance! He'll get me then, and I go t' hell."

"Trust me, it's gonna get worse, fast! Our deficit..."

"Do it yourself. No way I'm going anywhere near him."

"Sorry, I can't. You gave him the cube, so according to the *Supernatural Articles* you're the only one who can get it back."

"Right. He'll grab me, and you'll have my soul. No way."

The Devil gave him a hard look. "You've been listening to that hate propaganda, haven't you? I told you, it's all a pack of lies!"

"*You* should talk! They call you the Prince Of Lawyers! Why should I believe you?"

A smile flickered across the Devil's face. "That's one I hadn't heard. Look: hell is a nice place, really. I could show you, take you on a guided tour..."

"Not a chance!" he wheezed in fear. "You'd have me then!"

The Devil was becoming exasperated. "Webster, this is important. It's bigger than you and me. We have to get that cube back, and get immigration going again before our economy collapses. The people are counting on you! Please? For them?"

Webster fought down a faint trace of social consciousness, which wasn't difficult. "Why do I have to solve your problems? We have a deal, and I'm holding you to it."

"Even if it means living here? In your condition?"

"At least I'm not in hell!"

"You're not going to listen to reason?"

"I'm not going to listen to *you!*"

The Devil shook his head in despair. "This is not going to end well." He vanished.

§

March 5, 2145 AD

He was stirred out of his perpetual daze when something heavy landed on him. He struggled helplessly, but he was too weak to stand, much less shift the heavy roof beam. There was another loud crash; the building was collapsing! He cried out in terror, his voice lost amid the chorus of wailing.

It was several hours later when the heavy beam was shifted off him, revealing a dirty afternoon sky. Rough hands dragged him out of the wreckage and loaded him onto a crude cart with a dozen or more ancient bodies. More bodies were added, stacked up like sandbags until the cart groaned under the load. Only then did a couple dozen emaciated men take up the tow ropes and drag them slowly down a narrow street through a sea of crude shanties surrounding the dilapidated remains of the city's buildings. Everywhere Webster looked there were swarms of people; emaciated, hollow-eyed, dressed in rags. It reminded him of famine, of Bangladesh...of hell.

Eventually they came to another enormous warehouse. "We're full up," someone said. "They'll have to go somewhere else."

"Where? Th' whole porkin' city's full up."

There was a pause. "Alright, stick 'em wherever you can."

He was one of the last taken off the cart. "Hold up," the attendant said. "We can't take any more."

"There's no place else t' take him after th' place collapsed, and we can't just dump him on the street."

"Aw, hell. Stick him in the heater plant. There's a bit of room in there, and it's the only space we have left."

More rough hands dragged him off the cart and carried him bodily through the cavernous building. Everywhere he looked there were ancient bodies laying on metal cots stacked four high with barely enough room for the attendants to squeeze between. There must have been ten thousand in this one room alone, together with a few dozen emaciated workers dressed in rags to attend to them. He was carried through a narrow doorway into a dusty, ill-lit room, and placed on the floor next to a bulky heater unit. They left him there, alone.

Several hours later he felt that chilly aura again, which stirred him out of his senile haze. "So how's life these days?" the Devil asked.

His fears stirred along with his consciousness. "It's...living hell..."

"Trust me, you have no call to complain. We're in a full-blown recession. Unemployment is through the roof, businesses are folding, there's real suffering and misery in hell!"

"Not my problem. I don't live there."

"Have you no sense of humanity, Webster...okay, bad example. Webster, you're a part of this world. Just because people die and go to hell doesn't mean they can't strive for a little happiness in their lives. Those people are suffering; good people! They need your help to restore hell to what it's always been, to turn back the clock, to preserve something precious and rare. Isn't that worth dying for?"

He turned his head away. "I don't believe you!"

"Webster, Webster, Webster! Can't you see? Your mind has been poisoned by hate! Hell isn't what the fanatics say it is! Don't listen to their lies. It's not too late: you can save hell, and yourself, even now. Have a little faith, baby!"

"I'm not listening!"

The Devil sighed. "Oh, Webster, where did we go wrong?"

"Go away!"

"Honestly, I thought better of you, Webster. I only hope you see the error of your ways before your blindness destroys everything."

§

September 16, 2226 AD

They fed and tended to him indifferently for the next few years, but that faded away and eventually vanished, leaving him laying there forgotten. He starved. His weight dropped steadily until there was practically nothing left. By rights he should have died, but Death was...preoccupied...so he continued on in a not-quite-living-not-quite-dead state. At least he didn't lose any more weight, which was good since he was little more than skeletal.

The heating plant shut down at some point, leaving him at the mercy of the elements. The next winter was a hard one: he froze, solid, only to thaw out the next spring. He lapsed into suicidal despair; he went insane; he went catatonic. He came back and was sane again. He repeated that cycle several times over the years, and all the while he lay there next to the rusted hulk of the heating plant, too weak to move.

Who knows how long the horror went on? He lay there year after year staring sightlessly into the gloom. He cried. He cursed. He prayed. He bitterly denounced Death, the Devil, and himself for the mess he was in. He swore he would take the Devil's offer if given the change; hell couldn't be any worse than this. He swore he would never give in to the Devil, and would lay here forever; as horrid as his life was, at least he wasn't in hell. And so the years rolled by.

There came a day when the days were chilly and the nights frosty that he felt that faint *unnatural* aura again. The Devil's pseudo-life flowed into him, reviving him enough to speak.

"Why don't...you...quit bugging me?"

"I'd think you'd enjoy a little company," the Devil said, coldly. "So how's life these days?"

He struggled to lift his head. "Living...hell..."

The Devil knelt next to him. "Webster, I need your help. Our economy is a shambles, unemployment is out of sight, the budget is a disaster. *Please* take the cube back so Death can get to work again."

Just like that his wavering vanished. If the Devil could make his life this dreadful here in the living world, what must hell be like? "Never. You'll never...have me."

"Look, Webster, I appreciate how determined you are, but this is counterproductive. Standing on some crazy principle is all fine and dandy if you only hurt yourself, but your extremism is hurting countless innocents. Can't you unbend a little for the greater good?"

"I won't let you win! I won't submit to your hell! If I have to cripple your world, then so be it!"

"Honest," the Devil pleaded with him. "Hell beats this all hollow. In fact, we've been sending our troublemakers here. You're full of wrong-headed misconceptions about what hell is like. Won't you stop to reconsider? You're only hurting yourself and others with your unbending position!"

"If you screwed up the universe, it's your fault! I'm not going to die to maintain your standard of living. You came up with that cube, you cope with the consequences."

"People aren't dying out there! You have to *do* something!"

"It was...your idea. You figure it out."

"Look: I admit it. Giving you the cube was a *stupid* move on my part!" The Devil sounded genuinely annoyed with himself. "I figured if Death was...distracted...it would solve my problems with giving you immortality. Only it created an even bigger problem! *Please* help me straighten this mess out!"

"I've got my own problems, thanks to you."

The Devil sighed. "Always thinking of yourself. Don't you care about the hardships you've inflicted on others?"

"I've been a bit preoccupied, thanks to *you!*"

The Devil sobbed. "Webster, can't you forgive? I'm sorry! Trust me! Must I suffer forever for my foolish past?"

"You'll understand if I seem unmoved by your plight."

"Really, Webster! You are *such* an ingrate!"

§

December 5, 2385 AD

There was a chill wind blowing scattered snow flakes through the crumpled ruin of the heating plant, but he was too weak to even shiver in the cold. He lay where he'd lain for nearly four centuries, between the rusted hulk of the heating plant and the crumbling concrete wall of the heater room.

Eventually, at some timeless time after countless days had passed, he felt that strange aura filtering through him again. With it, he was able to stir, however faintly.

"Hello Webster. So how's life these days?"

"It's...living...hell..."

"You can end this misery," the Devil said, earnestly. "We've got a nice ground floor apartment all set up for you, with a lovely view of the bay. It's right on the trolley line. All you need to do is take that Rubik's Cube back."

His old fear came back with a vengeance: better this than damnation! "No...I won't let you have me."

"Webster, please: we're in a full-blown depression, and depression in hell is *some*thing!"

"You think I don't know about depression?"

"Look: things are bad. Trust me, life in hell is starting to live up to the rep. There's all sorts of political turmoil in hell these days...I might even be impeached. It's...it's..."

"It's hell?"

The Devil gave him a surly look. "*You* might say that!"

"You think anyone gives a damn for your political future?"

"Of course not! Why should they? They expect me to deliver, as they have every right to, and if I can't they have every right to vote me out. That's why I came here to appeal to your sense of duty, your sense of patriotism. We need the steady flow of souls to sustain our economy. Only you can turn the tap on again."

"These people's souls belong to them. Why should I help you take what's not rightfully yours?"

"Hell needs you! Even if you aren't a citizen yet, you can still do your part. Stand up and be counted; it'll guarantee your place as one of us!"

"You have your way of life, I have mine, they have theirs. Why should I change just to suit your vision of the perfect world?"

"I know you don't believe it, but hell is *worth* dying for."

"Says you! I don't see it that way!"

The Devil sighed. "So blind. You are *so* blind, Webster. You don't see the promise of hell right in front of you."

§

June 10, 2554 AD

It took Webster some time to realize someone was there in the room, and more to catch that faint, all too familiar aura. The not-quite-life flowed through him, and he was able to stir once more. "You again," he mumbled as he searched the shadows, trying to make out any movement.

"Yes, me again," the Devil said. "So how's life these days? I know: a living hell."

"You never give up?" he wheezed. "You came to...claim my soul? You can't have it! Not...while I'm still alive!"

The Devil knelt beside him close enough to be distinguished from the shadows. "Actually, I've decided to make you an offer you can't refuse. I'll release you from your bargain if, in return, you take the Rubik's Cube back from Death."

"You...?" Webster was stunned when he understood what the Devil said. "Why?"

"We have to get him back to work! This situation is totally out of hand. We're facing economic collapse! Why won't you *quit* with your obsessive obstruction and do something to help?"

"That's...not...*my* problem."

"Alright, you beat me! I admit it! Are you happy?" The Devil was frantic. "I don't know how you managed, but you've stonewalled until I have to concede defeat! I'd hoped for a couple centuries now that you'd grow tired of living and close the deal, but you're a stubborn cuss, so it looks like I have no choice but to cut you a deal to get things rolling again."

Honestly that was more tempting than Webster could express right then. He was mortally tired of immortality, and the only thing which kept him going all these years was his morbid fear of going to hell. But the Devil's offer to release him was slowly sinking in: if hell was off the table...

"Can...can I...go to heaven?" he managed.

He sensed rather than saw the Devil's frown. "Ah...no, not really. I'm afraid we're both in high stink right now. I wasn't able to persuade Him to let you in."

That figured. Webster managed to lift his head and gaze in Death's general direction. "What happens to me?"

"I'm sorry! Personally I'd say you're welcome to heaven, and good riddance! But you might say we're competitors, Him and me: He sets His own policies, and frankly He can be really anal at times. You wouldn't be happy there anyway, trust me."

"What happens to me?"

"Um...you wind up in limbo."

"Huh?"

"You'll be a ghost," the Devil said, reluctantly. "You'll remain here forever on the mortal plane. Sorry."

Webster's strength gave out, and his head sagged on the floor again. "A fat lot...of good...that'll do me."

"At least you won't suffer any more! You won't be hungry, and thirsty. You won't feel the cold, and you'll be able to move around. You could walk through walls, in fact. It's better than lying there for eternity!"

He was right about that, and Webster had had enough of immortality. He recalled, inanely, the comment made by the Devil five centuries ago: *"Sooner or later you'll get tired of living and decide to give up your immortality. We'll settle accounts then."* The Devil had him figured right from the beginning! Still, there was nothing for it. He was trapped right here in the living world as surely as if he was in hell. His only hope was to do the Devil's bidding and become a ghost haunting a desolate ruin.

He tried to sit up, but couldn't do more than stir his limbs vaguely. "I...can't move."

The Devil knelt over him, holding something. "I can help you. This is an Elixir Of Youth; it'll dial you right back to age twenty. You can do the job then."

Webster managed to focus on the palm-sized vial. An Elixir Of Youth, likely the one the Devil offered him five centuries ago. To be young and healthy again, if only for a few minutes. His will finally crumbled.

"Okay. You win." He tried to reach for it, but couldn't manage it. "...Can't...too weak..."

"Here, let me help you." The Devil held the vial to his lips. "I just want you to know there's no hard feelings."

§

126

It felt strange to be on his feet again, however faltering his steps. The potion performed as advertised: he was young, his joints worked, his eyes were clear, and aside from being weak with hunger, he hadn't felt this good since...since he couldn't remember when. Actually the elixir wasn't enough, and the Devil had to gift him with renewed health to overcome *centuries* of starvation. Webster was bemused by his solid arms and legs, his full face, and the slight gut he had when he was a youngster. Say what you like, the Devil delivered.

Death was standing a half mile away—where his living room once was—near a tumbled-down wall amid the remains of the large sheds built to house the *millions* of undying elderly. They were packed all around, shoulder to shoulder, head to toe; emaciated skeletons still living, still aware, laying under a sweltering summer sky. It was like a scene from the Holocaust. Webster faltered, sickened by the sight of living corpses stretching for miles amid the crumbled ruins.

"My...God...how many are there?"

"Hmm? Oh. The world population is over seventy billion. They're stacked up like cordwood all over the planet, and *you* complain about hell!"

"Seventy...billion," he whispered in horror. It was the most *monstrous* thing he could have imagined, something almost beyond comprehension. He turned to the Devil with a sweeping gesture. "Why? Isn't damnation bad enough?"

"This was your doing!" the Devil snapped. "Yes, the cube was what set this off, but *you* could have ended it five hundred years ago. These people suffer because of *your* stubbornness!"

Webster was appalled as that sank in. "I...never knew... I spent the last five centuries on my back. I thought they abandoned me to a living death long ago!" But now he saw the horrid truth: civilization had crumbled. *Seventy billion people!* They must be a solid carpet over every square inch of the planet. And they'd eaten *everything*. There wasn't a hint of green anywhere; no birds, no insects. There was no one to feed them and nothing to eat. The vast bulk of the human race were left to fend for themselves without food or shelter or any social organization whatsoever.

"Come on, get to it," the Devil hissed. "He has a backlog of at least thirty billion to process today alone. You can't *imagine* the immigration nightmare we'll be facing!"

"You think you got problems? My heart cries for you!"

Death glared at him with smoldering hatred as he worked the Rubik's Cube with a steady clatter of bare bones. Webster stood in front of him, steeling himself, feeling that horrid aura. Death's icy glare made him even more terrifying than before, chilling Webster to the bone just to look at him.

He was about to reach for the cube when a thought crossed his mind. He held back to ponder his options for a bit, looked Death square in the face, then turned to the Devil. "I'll want something first."

The Devil looked askance at him. "What is it now? Isn't this messed up enough already?"

"You want that cube? I want something in return."

The Devil did the Frustration Tango, he was so upset. "Alright! Whatever! Just do it!"

"I have your word?"

"Yes! Anything! Trust me! *Do* it!"

"Done!" Webster confronted Death again, and steeled himself for what he knew was coming. At least he had his youth back. A moment's hesitation, and he grabbed the cube. It slipped easily from Death's bony hands. Quick as lightning, Death grabbed his arm as he flinched...

...he felt a brief chill flow through him. Death relaxed his grip and shoved him away.

"Is...that it?" he asked after a moment.

"Yes," the Devil grumbled. "That wasn't so bad now, was it?"

"Um...no. I'm really dead?"

The Devil gestured, and Webster saw his young self lying on the crumpled pavement, lifeless. "Well I hope you're satisfied, after the mess you made."

"The mess *I* made? *You* dreamed up that damned cube!"

"Whatever. Now, if you'll excuse us, we have our work cut out for the next several centuries."

"Wait a minute! You made a promise! You owe me one."

The Devil fumed in frustration as Death shook his head in obvious dismay. "*Alright!* What*ever* it is, you're welcome to it, and I hope you choke on it!"

Webster pointed at Death. "I want his job."

"Um..." The Devil and Death exchanged bemused looks. "Come again?"

"I want his job. I want to be Death."

The Devil blinked in confusion as Death crossed his arms and glared at him. "You've lost me here. Why do you want *his* job?"

"You've said on several occasions how you get all the bad press; he's a great example of the problem. That getup is way over the top. You need a better image for this critical role."

"Um...?"

"Look at him! That rig's strictly out of the Dark Ages! It's no wonder people are afraid of dying!"

"It's Mesopotamian, actually." The Devil pondered him in confusion for a long moment. "So why do you want *his* job?"

"It used to be I was terrified of dying, in no small part due to *his* image, and yours." Webster sighed at his own long folly. "But lately you might say I've come to *appreciate* dying. I longed for it for *centuries*, in fact, so I know how it must be for all these people." He paraded his new, young physique. "Look at me: an average guy, not scary or terrifying. No black rags, no bony hands, just an ordinary Joe. I can ease the transition for the dying, offer a reassuring image to soothe their fears. If I'm gonna spend eternity wandering this world like a lost soul, I might as well get out and do something useful." He pondered the countless living corpses laying around them as far as the eye could see. "And I owe these people," he added with a shudder. "I had no idea..."

"Ah...hmmm." The Devil glanced back and forth between the two as he pondered that. "You have a point there, but I'm afraid it's not up to me. The position is a joint hire. We'd have to receive confirmation from up there." He gestured vaguely skyward.

Suddenly Webster was bathed in warm golden light. "Hmph!" the Devil grunted. "Isn't *that* something? We rarely agree on anything, but it looks like you got the job."

Death threw up his arms in disgust and walked away.

"I swear this is one for the ages," the Devil grumbled as he considered the devastation around them. "I ought to write a book. There's not many who can beat me, and you set a new standard. I guess you should be proud of that."

"Whatever." Webster remembered the Rubik's Cube he still held in his hand, and offered it to the Devil. "Here's this back."

"Like hell!" The Devil shuddered and fended it away. "Keep it, it suits you. Think of it as your symbol of office."

"Wonderful." Webster gazed around him in turn as he fiddled with the cube idly. Thirty *billion* to process. Today. What a *mess*. "I'd love to stay and chat, but I've got my work cut out for me for the next several centuries."

"You won't mess *this* up, will you?" the Devil asked. "Your record isn't exactly promising."

Webster gave him an annoyed glance. "Trust me."

*****

A Brief Note From The Author

Well, this was something different! I hope it was a good read for you. I would love to hear from you, my readers, to let me know how I am doing as an author. Every bit of input helps me to make my next effort a better product for your enjoyment.

All my best,

Bob Boyd

Available in print and Kindle from Amazon.
Visit our web site for details.

http://www.the-written-wyrd.org/shopping.shtml

*****

Titles from The Written Wyrd
2021-22

The Diplomacy Trilogy - Science fiction humor.
First contact from the aliens' perspective in a trio of lurid tell-all memoirs written by a team of alien diplomats sent to earth to open an embassy.

The MacKenna Trilogy - Science fiction military drama.
He was earth's greatest soldier; they needed his skills once more, but they didn't realize how wrong bringing him back from the dead was.

Nature's Way - Environmental disaster / apocalyptic horror.
This is the last day of our last stand against Nature out for revenge!

Trial - Science fiction political thriller.
The aliens demand justice for their murdered ambassador while right wing extremists plot revolution; which is the greater threat?

Overland - Period science fiction drama / romance.
He was trapped between a beautiful genetically enhanced revolutionary from the distant future and the inhuman monster sent to destroy her. Can he survive caught up in their titanic battle?

Playing God - Apocalyptic horror.
Brenda discovers she is the Dream Girl of a mad scientist capable of altering the past. Can she find a way to undo the disaster he wrought and prevent a nuclear holocaust?

The Big Snow - Environmental disaster / adventure.
A passenger train is wrecked at the top of Donner Pass in the worst storms in recorded history. Can the railroaders get the passengers to safety?

(continued)

Young Adult Demi-Novels:

Diplomacy's Children - YA humor / adventure.
>A young alien space fleet recruit faces his greatest challenge in a self-centered, foul-tempered human youngling he is ordered to keep in check.

Star Flight - YA adventure.
>She was an outcast, cursed with supernatural powers. She was offered a reprieve, a chance to start over, but could she survive the challenge?

Short Story Anthologies:

Deus Ex Machina - Humorous fantasy short story collection.
>From bungling wizards to moronic barbarians to redneck elves, here are the old tales of epic adventure as we would love to see them told - just once.

Ghoulish Good Fun - Macabre short story collection.
>Reality is a cruel practical joke. Laugh along with it if you dare!

*****

Available in print and Kindle from Amazon,
and in PDF and ePub downloads from Smashwords.
Visit our web site for details.

http://www.the-written-wyrd.org/shopping.shtml